Little white lies...big fat mess

Mary-Kate and Ashley
Sweet 16

Coming soon:

Little White Lies

By Carol Ellis

🎂 HarperEntertainment
An Imprint of HarperCollinsPublishers

A PARACHUTE PRESS BOOK

A PARACHUTE PRESS BOOK

Parachute Publishing, L.L.C.
156 Fifth Avenue, Suite 302
New York, NY 10010

Published by
HarperEntertainment
An Imprint of HarperCollins*Publishers*
10 East 53rd Street, New York, NY 10022-5299

ISBN 0-06-055647-1

First printing: October 2003

Printed in the United States of America

Visit HarperEntertainment on the World Wide Web at
www.harpercollins.com

10 9 8 7 6 5 4 3 2 1

chapter one

"Mary-Kate, why are you walking so funny?" my friend, Brittany Bowen, asked me. A bunch of us were hanging out at Click Café on Thursday afternoon, and I was goofing around.

"Funny? What do you mean?" I said, playing dumb. Clutching my coffee mug in both hands like a bouquet, I marched slowly toward the table where my sister, Ashley, was sitting with Brittany and some other friends.

Step, together, step, together.

Lauren Glazer, another one of my good friends, watched me. "You look sort of like a bride," she said.

I giggled and almost spilled my decaf coffee. "Close. Try brides*maid.*"

"Okay, brides*maid,*" Brittany said. "Is there a

wedding march playing somewhere that only you can hear?"

"No, I'm practicing." I set my mug on the table and squeezed onto the end of the bench next to our friend, Malcolm Freeman. "Didn't Ashley tell you?"

"Tell us what?" Ashley's boyfriend, Aaron Moore, asked.

"We're going to be bridesmaids in our cousin Jeanine's wedding next Saturday!" I announced.

"That is so cool!" Lauren exclaimed.

Brittany nodded, her beaded earrings brushing against her neck. "Why haven't we heard about this before?"

"We just found out yesterday," I said. "The wedding wasn't supposed to be for months. Now all of a sudden we've got only nine days!"

"They decided to move the date up because Jeanine's fiancé, James, just got a long overseas assignment," Ashley explained.

"What does he do?" Aaron asked.

"He's a reporter for *World Weekly Magazine*," I told him. "He's really nice and really cute—and *really* lucky! Jeanine is the coolest."

Ashley nodded. "She's ten years older than us, but she's like a big sister."

"She gives us advice about school and dating and clothes," I added.

"And she knows what she's talking about," Ashley said. "She's so together. She's a publicist for Unicorn Pictures."

Ben Jones, Lauren's boyfriend, broke into his lopsided grin. "The movie studio?"

Ashley nodded. "I hope I'm as successful as she is when I'm twenty-six."

"Don't worry, you will be," Aaron said. "You're so good at everything. And organized."

It's true. Ashley is extremely well-organized. And Aaron is so nuts about her, he actually thinks it's cute.

"I guess we'll find out in ten years," Ashley said. "But for now we've got tons to do before the wedding. Mom's throwing a coed shower for Jeanine this Saturday, at our house!"

Malcolm nudged me on the arm. "Let me out, Bridezilla," he said. "Sophie's here."

I scooted off the bench and waved to Malcolm's redheaded girlfriend. "Why doesn't she come sit with us?" I asked.

"Maybe your goofy bridesmaid walk scared her off," Malcolm said. He stood up, straightened his back, then settled into his usual slouch. "But

3

it's probably because she's in a hurry. She's leaving town with her parents tonight and"—he glanced at his watch—"I've got only ninety-four minutes to say good-bye."

"Better hurry then," I teased. "See you later."

As Malcolm slouched across the café, Sophie waved to us and smiled. Then she took his hand and the two of them left.

"He's hooked," Aaron said.

"Thanks to me," Ashley put in. She fixed up Malcolm and Sophie. "She's sweet, don't you think?"

"Very sweet," Brittany said.

I sat down next to her, stumbling over my backpack.

"Ashley, I almost forgot!" I said. "I stopped at home on my way here and I found these on the hall table." I unzipped the backpack and pulled out two thick, cream-colored envelopes.

"Ooh, our wedding invitations!" Ashley exclaimed. She ripped hers open and slid out the inner envelope. "Look at the writing—isn't it elegant? 'Ashley Olsen and Guest.'"

"You get to bring a date," Lauren said.

Ashley looked at Aaron. "Want to go to my cousin's wedding with me?"

Aaron made a face. "A wedding? Will I have to get dressed up?"

"No, not at all," Ashley teased. "It's a casual wedding, shorts and sneakers only." She gave him a playful punch on the arm. "Yes, you have to get dressed up! I bet you look great in a suit."

"Well, I'm the boyfriend," Aaron said. "I guess going to weddings is part of the job description."

"It will be fun," Ashley insisted.

I peeked at my invitation. Sure enough, it read *Mary-Kate Olsen and Guest*. Bringing a guest was no problem for Ashley. But I was boyfriend-less at the moment. Who was *I* going to bring?

Brittany nudged me. "What's the matter, Mary-Kate?"

"I'm just surprised, I guess," I said. "I didn't realize I'd need a date for the wedding."

"You don't *need* a date," Ashley told me. "It just means you can bring one if you want to."

"I would if I had one, but I don't," I said with a groan. "There isn't anybody I really want to ask, either."

"Then go by yourself," Brittany advised.

"But I'm afraid I won't have as much fun without a date," I admitted. "I mean, who will I dance with?"

Brittany rolled her eyes. "Use your imagination! Don't bridesmaids always walk down the aisle with an usher? Maybe yours will be cute. Anyway, I bet there'll be lots of single guys there."

"And a wedding is a great place to meet somebody," Lauren agreed.

Ashley nodded. "There's all that romance in the air."

"I never thought of that," I said. "Maybe there *will* be some cute guys there."

"Count on it," Brittany declared.

I hoped Brittany was right. I decided that being dateless really didn't matter. After all, this was my favorite cousin's wedding! How could I not have a great time? I was so happy for Jeanine that nothing—absolutely nothing—could ruin the day for me!

chapter two

"Look at this," I said to Ashley that night. I slid a photograph of Jeanine across the dining room table. "Her high school junior prom, remember?"

Mom decided to make a photo collage of Jeanine through the years for the wedding shower. So Ashley and I were going through a bunch of old albums and picking the best pictures.

"I remember that," Ashley said, looking at the photo. "She came by so we could all see her dress."

Mom walked in and plunked down two more albums. "These are the last of them, I think."

She peered over Ashley's shoulder. "That's a good one. I remember Jeanine was almost more excited about her new job than about the prom."

"She had a job?" Ashley asked.

Mom nodded. "For the summer, working in a law office."

"I wish I could find something like that," Ashley said. "I really want to get a part-time job. As soon as this wedding craziness is over, I'm going to start looking."

The phone rang and Mom hurried toward the kitchen. "That's either your aunt Katherine or the caterer," she said.

"Wedding craziness is right," I said. "Every time the phone rings, it's Aunt Katherine or Jeanine with a new seating arrangement."

Aunt Katherine is Jeanine's mom and our mother's sister.

Ashley nodded, then burst out laughing. "Look, Mary-Kate!" she said, sliding an album over for me to see. "Our famous three-family camping trip to Sequoia National Park! Remember that?"

"It's burned into my memory forever," I said, checking out the pictures.

Eight years ago our family, Jeanine's family, and another family, the Harrises, had gone on a week long camping trip together. It would have been perfect, except for . . .

"George!" I cried. I pointed to a photo of an eight-year-old boy.

George was the same age as Ashley and me. His yellow-blond hair flopped over his forehead and his small blue eyes squinted against the sun. "Obnoxious George Harris!"

"He was awful, wasn't he?" Ashley said. She glanced over her shoulder to make sure Mom didn't overhear. Mom and Aunt Katherine were still good friends with the Harrises. "Remember the pinecones in our sleeping bags?"

"I remember everything he did to us," I said. "Chasing us with that fake snake, dunking us in the lake, griping about everything, and those horrible temper tantrums—"

I broke off and took a deep breath. "He was the biggest pest I ever met!"

"I know," Ashley said. "I couldn't stand him either. Hey, I wonder if he'll be at the wedding?"

"Don't even think it," I said with a shudder.

"We haven't seen him in years," she said. "Maybe he's changed by now."

"I'm sure he has," I agreed. "For the worse!"

The doorbell rang, and a few seconds later Jeanine stuck her head around the dining room door. She smiled at Ashley and me. "Hi, you guys! Your dad told me you'd be in here."

"Hi, Jeanine!" I said, smiling back at her as

she came over to the table. She looked great, as usual, her green eyes twinkling with excitement.

"Want to see some pictures of you that we picked for the photo collage?" Ashley asked.

"Sure!" Jeanine tossed a stiff sheet of poster board onto the table and sat down. "It's so nice of your mom to host the shower for me."

"She loves doing it," I told her. I pointed to one of the photos. "Look, there you are winning some kind of prize."

Jeanine glanced at it. "That was the seventh grade speech prize. Look at those braces!" She groaned.

"They gave your smile a real sparkle," I teased.

"Is that the seating chart?" Ashley asked, pointing to Jeanine's poster board. Colored name tags were stuck all over it.

"Right, for the wedding reception," Jeanine said. "It's almost finished, but I want to check with your mom about where to put a couple of her friends. That's why I stopped by."

"She's on the phone," I said, pointing toward the kitchen. "Want me to tell her you're here?"

Jeanine shook her head. "I'm going to sit still while I have the chance. I've been so busy since we moved the wedding date."

"Mary-Kate, look!" Ashley said. "Guess who's coming to the wedding." She turned the seating chart around and pointed to a name.

"'George Harris,'" I read. "Oh, no! Please don't tell me he's at our table."

"George Harris?" Mom asked, coming in from the kitchen. "What a coincidence! That was his mother on the phone. We were just talking about him."

She gave Jeanine a kiss on the cheek and smiled at me. "Guess what, Mary-Kate?"

"What?" I asked.

"Mrs. Harris told me that George doesn't have a date for the wedding. And when she found out you were planning to go by yourself—"

A warning bell went off in my head. This didn't sound good. . . .

"—she said wouldn't it be fun if the two of you went together," Mom continued. "I told Mrs. Harris you'd be happy to. So now you have a date for the wedding after all!"

"You *what*?" I cried. "Mom! How could you do that without even asking me?"

"George just got back from boarding school and he doesn't know anyone out here," Mom said. "And you don't have a boyfriend at the moment,

11

right, Mary-Kate? So this is the perfect solution!"

My stomach sank as Mom took George's name tag and stuck it next to mine. Mom might not see any problem, but I could see plenty—like George making me miserable at my cousin's wedding!

I glanced at Ashley. She looked sympathetic, but I needed more than sympathy. I needed a way out of this, fast! But I didn't want to hurt Mom's feelings. I knew she was trying to help.

"Mom, wait!" I said. "George can't be my date because . . . I have a new boyfriend!"

Ashley's eyebrows shot up and her mouth dropped open. Fortunately, Mom didn't notice or she would have known I was lying.

"You do?" Mom asked.

I nodded and glanced at Ashley again. She closed her mouth, but she still looked shocked.

"Why haven't you told me about him?" Mom asked.

"Oh, well, we just met," I said, crossing my fingers.

"That's wonderful," Mom said. "Who is he? What's his name?"

"Yeah, who's the lucky guy?" Jeanine asked.

Good question, I thought. "Billy," I said, blurting out the first name that popped into my head.

"What's he like?" Mom asked.

"Oh, he's . . . cute. And smart," I added. "He's captain of the debate team."

This was kind of fun, actually. Since Billy didn't exist, I could make him anything I wanted.

"And he likes to rock climb and he totally loves acoustic guitar," I said.

"When can we meet him?" Mom asked.

"Ummm . . . soon," I said.

The phone rang.

"That must be Katherine," Mom said, checking her watch. "She said she'd call. Come on, Jeanine, let's get this seating chart finished—once and for all!"

The second Mom and Jeanine were out of earshot, Ashley leaned across the table. "What do you think you're doing?" she asked. "There's no rock-climbing debater named Billy!"

"Shhh!" I glanced toward the kitchen door. "I know it was a lie, but I was desperate! Besides, Mom doesn't ever have to know. I've got it all figured out."

"What do you mean?" Ashley whispered.

"I'll keep pretending that I have a boyfriend right up until the wedding," I said. "That will give George plenty of time to find another date. Then, on the morning of the wedding, I'll tell Mom that Billy and I broke up. I'll be in the clear and nobody will be hurt by my little white lie."

"Good news, Mary-Kate!" Mom said, coming back into the dining room with Jeanine. "I checked the plans for the shower and there's room for one more person. You can invite Billy!"

I gulped. "To the wedding shower?"

Mom nodded. "It's coed, so the whole family can meet him!"

"Uhhh, sure." I pasted on a smile, but inside I was panicking again. Now what was I going to do?

The shower was only *two days* away! How was I going to find a boyfriend by then?

"I just don't get it, Mary-Kate," I said as I followed her into the school's Website office the next morning. "What are you going to tell Mom when 'Billy' doesn't show up at the shower?"

Mary-Kate sat down in front of a computer and switched it on. "Who says Billy won't show up?" she asked with a grin.

"Sorry, but have you totally lost it? You made Billy up!" I reminded her. "He doesn't exist!"

"Want to bet?" she said. "I know he's out there somewhere and I'm going to find him!"

She tapped some keys, and Love Link, my matchmaking program, appeared on the monitor's screen.

I invented a special matchmaking system one day during math class. After a while, it got so popular that I put in on the school Website. Kids who log on to Ashley's Love Link fill out a questionnaire and post their photos. Then they scan through the other photos and questionnaires until they find someone they are interested in.

"I have it all figured out," Mary-Kate said, scrolling down the screen.

"That's what you said yesterday before Mom invited Billy to the shower," I told her.

"I know, but this plan is Mom-proof," Mary-Kate declared. "First I search the files for the Billys. Then all I have to do is find one to take to the shower and the wedding. It'll be a snap."

"Oh, right," I joked. "Finding a debater named Billy who's into rock climbing and acoustic guitar by tomorrow night? No problem!"

"Okay, maybe it won't exactly be a snap," Mary-Kate admitted. She pointed to the monitor. "But I know he's in here, so don't just stand there,

Ashley! You've got to help me find him! Right now!"

I sat down at another computer and called up Love Link. I wasn't as sure as she was that the perfect Billy existed. But if he did, we had to find him—fast.

chapter three

"I can't wait to see our dresses!" I exclaimed to Mom and Mary-Kate that night.

We had just arrived at the bridal boutique for our first fitting. It was a small shop, very posh-looking, with soft lighting and comfortable couches.

Jeanine and Aunt Katherine were already there with three women about Jeanine's age. As Mom went off to talk to Aunt Katherine, Jeanine brought the others over to us.

"Ashley, Mary-Kate, meet my other bridesmaids," Jeanine said. "This is Diane, Lainie, and Alyssa. We were suitemates all four years at college. These are my two favorite cousins," she added, smiling at Mary-Kate and me.

"I remember you," Mary-Kate said to Diane, a

tall woman with curly brown hair. "You came to our house for Thanksgiving once."

Diane nodded. "Jeanine brought me home our freshman year. I'm surprised you remember. You were only, what? Seven?"

"Eight," I told her. "But it's impossible to forget the year of the Deep-Fried Turkey Disaster."

"Anybody hungry?" Lainie said. "I see some coffee and pastries over there." She pointed to a low table across the room.

"I wouldn't mind a cup of coffee," Alyssa said. She and Diana followed Lainie to the table.

"Mmmm—mini-eclairs!" Lainie smiled, showing deep dimples in her round cheeks. She popped one into her mouth.

"Oh, good, here's Ava," Jeanine said, nodding toward the door.

A slender and intense-looking woman walked into the boutique. She wore a black suit and had a cap of frosted blond hair.

"I don't believe it!" I gasped. "That's *the* Ava!"

"Who's Ava?" Mary-Kate asked.

"She's only the best wedding planner in L.A.," I said. "She's famous for her 'glitch-free' weddings. She does celebrity weddings, too. I've read lots of magazine articles about her."

Jeanine nodded. "When we moved the wedding date up, I knew I'd need a planner, and Ava's the best."

"Totally," I agreed. Every wedding Ava did was a mega-success. People talked about her magic touch, but I knew it wasn't magic. It was planning and organizing, right down to the tiniest detail.

Ava strode up. "Hello, Jeanine. How are the dresses? Have you tried them on yet?"

"Not yet," Jeanine replied. She introduced Mary-Kate and me. Ava smiled at us and quickly got down to business.

"We need to order the cake ASAP, so let's choose a bakery right now," she told Jeanine, pulling a Palm Pilot from her black shoulder bag. "Tell me what you think of these."

Ava read off the names of three bakeries.

Jeanine shook her head at the first two. "My mom and I went for tastings at the first two places. Their cakes weren't that great," she said. "And I've never heard of Gateaux."

"It's fairly new," Ava told her. "I'll have them fax me some customer references before we decide."

Ava sounded calm, but when I saw the tiny frown line between her eyes, I knew she was stressed. A wedding cake is a major production. You can't order it a couple of days before the ceremony.

"I know a great place," I said. "The Cakery. They did Mary-Kate's and my sweet sixteen cake and it was spectacular-looking."

"And spectacular-tasting," Mary-Kate added.

"Great!" Jeanine exclaimed. "Thanks, Ashley."

"Yes, good suggestion," Ava told me. "What's the name again? I'll look it up when I get back to my office."

"The Cakery. But you don't have to look it up," I replied. "I have all the information with me." I dug into my bag and pulled out my glittery purple notebook. "Here," I said, flipping to the right page. "Name, phone number, contact person."

"Perfect," Ava said, entering the info into her Palm Pilot.

"Oh, and I have references, too," I added. "I can fax them to you if you like. They're all excellent."

"I'll take your word for it," Ava said. "Thanks again, Ashley. I'm impressed with your organization."

"Organization is Ashley's middle name," Mary-Kate said.

"I like that." Ava smiled at me. "I could use an intern like you."

An intern! I jumped at the idea. "I'd be happy to help with anything," I told her.

Ava chuckled. "Better watch out—I might take you up on that offer."

"I'm serious," I told her. "You can trust me to get things done. You just saw how organized I am. I'm really good at planning and taking care of details."

Ava stared at me thoughtfully, then gave a decisive nod. "Let's try it," she said. "Since you're still in school, you can start by helping me with Jeanine's wedding."

"That will be perfect!" I said. "This is going to be such a great experience!"

"Well, if it works out, it might lead to a summer job," Ava said. "I'm already considering some other high school kids, so I'll add your name to the list."

A job! I was so excited I could barely say "thank you." I was actually going to be working with *the* Ava! How awesome was that?

"Isn't this great, Mary-Kate?" Ashley asked as

Ava and Jeanine sat down to go over more details. "I'm going to be Ava's intern!"

"Yeah, never again will I make fun of your purple notebook," I joked.

The shop door opened, and another woman walked in. It took me a minute to recognize her. But once I did, my heart sank.

"Oh, no, Ashley," I whispered. "Look who just came in."

Ashley glanced across the room. "It's Mrs. Harris!"

I nodded. Obnoxious George's mother. What was she doing at the fitting? Then I noticed the little girl trailing behind her. She was about four or five, with the same thick blond hair and blue eyes as George.

"Oh, yeah," I murmured, remembering now. "Mrs. Harris had a baby about four years ago. That must be George's little sister."

"She looks a lot like George," Ashley said. "Only cuter."

Mrs. Harris took the little girl's hand and pulled her over to Mom. "Regina, you know Mrs. Olsen," she said.

"Hi, sweetie." Mom gave Regina a hug.

My mom runs a day-care center and she's

really great with kids. "You're going to be a flower girl, aren't you? Are you excited?"

"She's thrilled," Mrs. Harris said. "Regina loves pretty dresses."

"Ah-ha!" I muttered to Ashley. "So that's why Mrs. Harris is here."

"Okay, everybody, the fitters have everything ready for you," Jeanine called out. "Come on back with me."

We hurried into the dressing rooms, eager to see what we'd be wearing for Jeanine's big day.

"They're so beautiful!" Ashley exclaimed.

"Really gorgeous." I took my dress from the fitter and held it up. It was a simple ankle-length silk slip dress in a deep shade of blue. "I love the color!"

"I'm glad," Jeanine said. "I wanted something dramatic, but I worried that it might be too dark."

"No, it's perfect," I said.

"Good. Oh—I have a photo of your bouquets." Jeanine hurried to the door. "Be right back!"

I quickly slipped out of my clothes and into the bridesmaid dress. It was too long, but otherwise it fit perfectly, and so did Ashley's.

"You two look beautiful," Mom said proudly. She'd come in with Mrs. Harris and Regina. Regina's dress was the same color as ours, but in a "little-girl" style with a wide sash and puffed sleeves.

I grinned. "You're not just saying that because you're our mother, are you?"

"Of course I am," Mom admitted. "But you still look beautiful."

"Your mother's right," Mrs. Harris said, hurrying after Regina, who was getting ready to do a somersault in her dress.

"She really is," Diane, one of the other bridesmaids, agreed.

"Thanks," I said. "But who wouldn't look good in this?"

At that moment, Lainie emerged from behind one of the small, curtained dressing areas.

I suddenly wished I'd kept my mouth shut.

"I look awful!" Lainie cried.

Maybe not awful, I thought. *But definitely not good.* I couldn't quite figure out what the problem was, but the dress was just totally wrong on her.

Lainie twisted and turned in front of the mirror. "How come the rest of you look so great and I look like I'm wearing a sack?"

"Nobody's going to pay that much attention to you, Lainie," Alyssa told her. "The bride's the main attraction."

"I don't care," Lainie said, blinking back tears. "I wanted to look pretty."

"You *are* pretty," Ashley declared. "And the color is perfect on you—it matches your eyes."

Lainie peered into the mirror. "It does, doesn't it?"

"That's the first thing I noticed," Ashley told her.

"Well . . ." Lainie took another look at herself and finally smiled. "Maybe I don't look so bad after all."

"You look great," Ashley said firmly.

Great? The color might match Lainie's eyes, but she still looked like she had on a sack. At least she felt better, though, thanks to Ashley.

"Here it is," Jeanine said, coming back into the dressing room with a photograph. "This is what your bouquets will be like. Baby roses—my favorite flower."

After we all admired the bouquet, it was time to get our dresses pinned for alterations. Ashley and I stepped up onto two side-by-side boxes and the seamstresses started pinning.

Mom and Mrs. Harris sat down on a nearby couch. Regina had changed back into her regular clothes and sat cross-legged on the floor.

25

Mrs. Harris gave the little girl a butter cookie, then smiled at me. "Mary-Kate, I was really hoping that you and George would be going to the wedding together."

"Well, it would have been nice. . . ." I gave a regretful little shrug. "But I can't wait for everyone to meet Billy at the shower tomorrow night."

"Oh, yes, I can't either," Mom put in.

Ashley caught my eye. "*Is* there a Billy for us to meet?" she mumbled under her breath.

I gave her a thumbs-up. We were facing each other on the boxes, and I leaned close. "I just found him this afternoon," I whispered. "His Love Link profile was perfect, so I called him. He's meeting me tomorrow afternoon at Click for sort of a screening."

"He actually said yes?"

I nodded. "He sounded really nice."

Ashley shook her head doubtfully. "I sure hope you know what you're doing, Mary-Kate. This sounds too easy."

"Will you stop worrying?" I whispered. "All I have to do is get through tomorrow night! What could be easier than that?"

chapter four

"A problem?" I said to Ava on the phone Saturday morning. "Not with the bakery, I hope."

"No, no, a problem with time." Ava spoke in a clipped tone. I could just see her checking her watch. "I don't have enough of it, so I need you to do something for me."

"Sure!" I rushed over to my desk and grabbed my notebook and a pen. "I'm ready for anything," I said, perching on the desk chair. My first assignment!

"Okay, here's the deal: The bakery needs the money by closing today or they won't guarantee the cake in time, but I'm stuck in a meeting." Ava stopped and took a breath. "I need you to stop by my office and get the check, then drive it over to the bakery. Got a pen?"

I held up my pen as if she could see it. "Got one."

As Ava rattled off the directions to her office in Beverly Hills, Mary-Kate came into my room. She started to say something, but I held up a hand.

"Third floor, Suite Two, Jenna," Ava said.

"Jenna," I muttered, scribbling as fast as I could.

Mary-Kate checked out the top of my dresser.

"She's at the front desk, get the check from her," Ava told me.

"Okay, and—"

"And that's it, gotta go, thanks," Ava said hurriedly.

"Ashley, where are—" Mary-Kate started to say when I hung up.

"Wait just a second," I told her, scanning my notes. "That was Ava, and I need to make sure I can read everything she told me. She talked so fast!"

Mary-Kate waited until I looked up from the notebook. "Where are the car keys?" she asked.

"In my—" I stopped short. "No. Sorry, Mary-Kate. You can't have the car."

"What do you mean? It belongs to both of us," Mary-Kate reminded me.

"I know," I said.

Our parents had given us a pink Mustang convertible for our sixteenth birthday. "But we made a deal—when we both want the car at the same time, whoever needs it most gets it."

"Exactly. And I need it the most right now."

"No, *I* need it the most," I told her. "I have to drive over to Ava's office, pick up the cake check, and then drive the check all the way across the city to the bakery."

"But I'm meeting Billy at Click this afternoon!" Mary-Kate said.

"Can't you change the time?"

"Ashley, the shower is tonight!" Mary-Kate reminded me. "I have to meet him this afternoon or I'll be bringing a complete stranger to the shower as my date! And that will never work."

"Well, I have to get the check to the bakery on time," I argued. "I can't goof up on Ava's very first assignment! My summer job is on the line!"

"Okay, look. Why don't you drop me off at Click before you do your errand for Ava?" Mary-Kate suggested, sighing in frustration. "That's fair, right?"

"Uh . . ." I did some fast mental math. "No. I can't."

"Why not?" Mary-Kate cried. "You're getting the car. All you have to do is give me a ride to Click!"

"It's too far away from Ava's office," I told her. "If I take you there, I'll never get to the bakery before it closes. And it closes really early on Saturday."

"Ashley, please!" Mary-Kate wailed.

"Hey, you two, what's wrong?" Mom's voice called from down the hall.

"Nothing, Mom," Mary-Kate called back, giving me a pleading "don't-say-a-word" look.

"From what I heard, it sure didn't sound like nothing." Mom appeared in my doorway with an armful of clean laundry. "What's the problem?"

I explained about my errand for Ava. "She's counting on me, and I want to do the job right. Besides, it's not just any cake, it's Jeanine's wedding cake."

Mom dumped a pile of T-shirts and shorts onto my bed and glanced at Mary-Kate. She was waiting for her to say why *she* needed the car.

I was waiting, too. Would she finally tell the truth about Billy?

Mary-Kate leaned against my desk and crossed her arms. "Well . . ." she said, taking a deep breath. "I have to have the car because I'm meeting Billy."

I groaned to myself. *Billy still lives*, I thought.

"Well, I'm sorry, Mary-Kate, but that doesn't sound quite as urgent as Ashley's errand," Mom said.

Mary-Kate stared at her feet. "I know, but, um . . . it's not just a date, it's . . ."

"I mean, if it was a matter of life or death," Mom went on, "I could understand, but—"

"Well, it is, sort of," Mary-Kate said.

I had to stop myself from rolling my eyes. A matter of life or death? Puh-leeze!

"I—I promised I'd help him with a food drive," Mary-Kate finally said. She leaned down and picked up a yellow thread from the floor. I knew she couldn't look Mom in the eye. "At the community center. So it *is* important."

Too bad it's not true, I thought. I poked her in the arm, but she ignored me.

"Anyway, that's why we were arguing about the car," she said, twisting the thread around her finger.

"Hmmm. I see the problem," Mom said. "Well, Ashley, why don't you just drop Mary-Kate off? The community center's on your way to Ava's office, isn't it?"

"Yes, but . . ."

Mom gave me one of her "don't-argue" looks. "All you have to do is pull up and let your sister out. Now, I have a million more things to do for tonight, so I'll see you two later."

As soon as Mom left the room, I jumped up and pulled a green T-shirt from the pile of laundry. "Thanks a lot, Mary-Kate!"

"I'm sorry," she said.

I took off my pink shirt and pulled on the green one. "Now I'm stuck driving you to Click," I told her. "And it's *not* on my way. It's all the way across town!"

"I know. I'm sorry," Mary-Kate repeated. "But I just have to meet Billy!"

"And I have to get the money to the bakery!" I reminded her, checking my hair out in the dresser mirror. "How am I supposed to do that? Fly?"

"You'll figure out a way," Mary-Kate replied.

"Sure." I grabbed my backpack and stuffed my cell phone and notebook into it. "I could always tell Mom the truth."

"Ashley, you can't!" Mary-Kate gasped. "I know you're mad and I don't blame you, but please, please, don't rat me out! I'll let you have dibs on the car for a month. I'll fold your laundry for a year! I'll—"

"Stop!" I couldn't help laughing a little. It was hard to stay mad at her for long. "I'm not going to tell, okay?"

"Thank you, thank you, thank you!"

"You're welcome. But, Mary-Kate, you'd better be careful," I warned. "All these little white lies could get you in big trouble."

"It's almost over," Mary-Kate said. "Once I get through tonight, everything can go back to normal."

I hoped so. But I had my doubts.

"Are you all right, miss?" the manager at The Cakery asked me.

I nodded and tried to catch my breath. "Couldn't find . . . a good parking spot," I gasped. "Had to run . . . before you closed."

I gave the manager Ava's check and leaned against the counter while he went over the order. I glanced at the big clock on the wall. Two minutes till closing time. Thanks to a shortcut I found, I'd just made it!

"Everything's in order," the manager said. "The cake will be ready next Saturday."

"Great!" I said. "Thanks."

I was so relieved. If I had been just two minutes later, Jeanine wouldn't have had a wedding cake—and my first assignment for Ava would have been a total disaster.

To celebrate, I bought a lemon pastry and ate it as I walked back to the car. My cell phone rang on the way. It was Ava. "Hi, Ashley. Tell me you got the check to the bakery."

"I got the check to the bakery," I said.

Ava sighed with relief. "Good job! I forgot to tell you the bakery closed early. I wasn't sure you'd make it."

Neither was I, I decided not to say. "Jenna met me downstairs with the check, and that saved some time. Everything's taken care of," I assured her.

"That's great, Ashley. Listen, I have another assignment for you if you're free tomorrow."

"I'm definitely free," I told her, jumping at the chance.

"Good. Stop by my office tomorrow about noon," Ava said. "This one's as important as the cake, so don't let me down."

"Don't worry, I'll be there," I promised. "You can count on me!"

chapter five

"Excuse me, is your name Billy?" I asked a muscular guy sitting at a table in Click.

The guy glanced up from his magazine and shook his head. "Sorry."

Me too, I thought. He was cute. He was alone. And he looked like he could scramble up the side of a mountain without breaking a sweat.

Maybe if the "real" Billy didn't show up, I thought, I could talk this guy into playing the role. I bought a lime soda and found a place to sit.

"Mary-Kate?" A boy popped up as I passed by. His bony knees bumped the table and his grape drink sloshed out of the glass. "I'm Billy Foster. Well, William. Actually, I like to be called Will. But you can call me Billy. Anyway, we talked on the phone yesterday."

Thunk! My heart sank as I watched him mop up the purple mess with a wad of napkins. This guy was short and thin and pale. Nobody would ever believe he climbed rocks.

Billy finished mopping up and smiled shyly. He had brown hair and soft brown eyes.

"Thanks for coming," I said, pulling out a chair.

"No problem." He gave me another bashful smile. "It's cool to meet you. I've wanted to talk to you at school lots of times."

"Really? Why didn't you?"

He ducked his head. "Oh, you know. You're a junior, I'm a freshman."

A freshman! His Love Link profile didn't say that!

"I was kind of surprised when you called and asked me for a date," he said.

"Well, it's not exactly a date. . ." I began. How could I explain it to him? I didn't want to insult him—he might leave. And I was desperate.

"It's my cousin's wedding shower," I went on. "It's tonight, and it would be great if you could come."

"Sure! I'd really like that, Mary-Kate." His brown eyes got even softer as he gazed at me.

Uh-oh. Did Billy have a crush on me? All I

wanted was a date for my cousin's wedding shower!

"Cool," I said cheerfully. "Maybe we should get to know each other a little. What are you interested in?"

"I collect baseball cards," he said. "And I like to watch wrestling."

Wrestling? "That's great," I said. "But, um, you don't happen to play the acoustic guitar, do you?"

"No . . . We learned to play the recorder in elementary school. But I don't really remember much about it."

Not helpful. "That's nice. But what about the guitar? I mean, you like it, right?"

"I guess so," he said. "I never really thought about it before. Do you play?"

"No," I said. "I just like people who like the acoustic guitar. But forget about that. How about rock climbing? Ever been?"

He was beginning to look confused. I couldn't blame him. "Rock climbing? No way. I'm afraid of heights." He paused. "I guess you're really into it, huh?"

"Not really," I admitted. "I've never done it. I just thought you might have . . ." I let the sentence trail off. There wasn't much point in finishing it.

"I don't suppose you've done much community service," I said. "Food drives, stuff like that?"

He shook his head. "I like to *eat* food. Does that help?"

"Hmm . . . What about the debate team?" I asked. "Ever have an argument with somebody?"

"There's a debate team?"

I sighed. He was trying so hard to please me. But so far, Billy was the total opposite of the guy I made up.

There was nothing I could do. It was too late to find a new and improved Billy. I had to make this one work, somehow.

At least there's one good thing about him, I decided as he flashed me another puppy-dog smile. He won't have to fool anybody about how much he likes me!

"I'll get it!" I called when the doorbell rang that evening. The shower didn't start for an hour. Maybe it was another gift delivery for James and Jeanine.

"Hi, Ashley," the boy on the porch said. He was a head shorter than me, with big brown eyes. I'd never seen him before.

"Hi, um . . ." I said.

"I'm Will Foster," he told me.

The name didn't sound familiar. "Will?"

"Mary-Kate calls me Billy," he explained.

No way! I thought. This short, skinny boy could not possibly be the amazing Billy!

"Hi, Billy!" Mary-Kate cried, running up behind me in her gauzy lavender halter dress. "Come on in."

"Wow, Mary-Kate," Billy said, tripping over the doorstep as he came inside. "You look totally amazing."

"Thanks." Mary-Kate forced a grin in my direction. "I guess you already met Billy."

I nodded and gave her a look that said "are you crazy?" She shrugged and grinned even harder.

Billy peered into the living room. Mom had decorated it with tons of flowers, the photo collage, and a big banner that read "Good Luck, Jeanine and James."

"Am I the first one here?" he asked.

"The very first," I told him. Our parents weren't even here. Mom had to make a run for extra napkins. Dad is an executive at Zone Records and he's always working late. He'd probably get home just before the party started.

"I asked Billy to come early so we could talk a little more," Mary-Kate explained. "Did you know he's going out for the football team next year, Ashley?"

This little guy? Playing football? I shook my head. "What position?" I asked.

"Equipment manager," Billy said.

"Oh." I plastered a smile on my face. "That's great."

"I bet he'll get it, too," Mary-Kate said.

Sure, why not? There wasn't much competition for those equipment manager spots.

"Mary-Kate, Mom asked us to get some serving bowls ready," I said. "Could you give me a hand in the kitchen?"

"Sure," Mary-Kate said. "I'll be right back, Billy."

She followed me into the kitchen. "Please tell me you're not going through with this," I whispered.

"What do you mean?"

"Mary-Kate!" I held up my fingers and started counting. "One, no way will anyone believe he's your boyfriend. I mean, he's nice, I guess, but he's just totally wrong. How old is he anyway?"

"Umm . . . fourteen," she mumbled.

I sighed. "Two, he's obviously no rock climber. Does he at least play the guitar?"

"No," she admitted. "But I thought he could say he's too busy with the football team."

"Three," I said. "Why do I get the feeling he's not on the debating team? Mary-Kate, what are you going to do? This could be a bigger disaster than going to the wedding with George!"

"I know, I know!" Mary-Kate groaned. "I thought I could make it work, but it's impossible. I have to get rid of him now, before Mom or Dad see him."

"But you invited him to the party!" I said. "How can you kick him out of the house now?"

"I don't know!" she groaned again. "Help me think of something!"

I checked my watch as Ashley and I hurried out of the kitchen. Forty minutes to go. Could we get rid of Billy in time?

He smiled as we came into the living room. I smiled back and took a deep breath. "Sorry we took so long," I told him. "Ashley suddenly got a killer headache and I had to find the aspirin."

"I think I have a fever, too," Ashley murmured weakly. "I hope I'm not coming down with that weird flu."

"I heard about that," I said darkly. "It starts with a headache and fever."

"And the chills," Billy added. "I heard about it, too."

"Uh-oh. I'm definitely shivering." Rubbing her arms, Ashley sank onto the couch next to Billy. "I think I've got it."

"Don't get too close to her, Billy," I said. "It's supposed to be incredibly contagious."

"Yeah, but it lasts only twelve hours." Billy stood up and walked over to the photo collage, which was propped on a big easel.

I gave Ashley a helpless look. So much for scaring him off with germs.

"I guess I'll be meeting everybody, huh?" Billy said, scanning the photos.

Not if I can help it, I thought, joining him at the collage. As I looked at the pictures, I had a brainstorm. "Yes, but don't worry."

"Why should I worry?"

"Well, you know how families are," I told him. "They all have a few weirdos. See him?" I pointed to a photo of Jeanine's uncle Brad, one of the

42

sweetest men I'd ever met. "We call him Brad the Mad. Secretly, of course."

Ashley coughed loudly.

"Oh, and don't let Libby bother you," I went on, pointing to a picture of Jeanine's great-aunt, who never bothered anybody. "She takes being an agent a little too seriously."

"Agent? FBI? CIA?" Billy asked.

"Nobody knows for sure," I whispered. "But she'll definitely give you the third degree. And then there's Dave."

Ashley coughed again. There was no Dave. I hoped she didn't ask me who he was.

"Dave's picture isn't here," I said. "He has this phobia about being photographed. Probably because of all the mug shots."

Billy raised his eyebrows. Was he starting to look nervous?

Sorry, Brad and Libby, I thought. *I love you both, but I have to get rid of Billy!*

"I just wanted to warn you," I said, crossing my fingers. "My family can be a little strange. If you don't want to stay, I won't blame you."

"Oh, that's okay." Billy chuckled. "I've got weird relatives too. Besides, I wouldn't skip out on our date."

"I heard a car!" Ashley cried, hopping to her feet.

"Speedy recovery," Billy commented as Ashley ran to the front window.

"It's Dad!" Ashley reported. "And Mom's right behind him!"

"Stay in here!" I told her. I pulled Billy into the kitchen, thinking fast. I couldn't let Mom and Dad meet him or they'd know I'd been lying. But what could I say? Should I try something radical, like the truth?

"Billy, I have a confession to make," I said.

I took a deep breath and quickly explained the situation—the short version. "I-I don't think I really need a date for the shower after all."

"What do you mean?" he asked, blinking his puppy dog eyes.

"It's not your fault," I said, having a major guilt attack. "Tonight's date just won't work."

"Well, okay," he said. "I don't really get it. But if tonight's not good, what about another night? I mean, I was really looking forward to going out with you. And I sort of bragged to my friends about how you like me."

"I *do* like you!" I said. Actually, I did. Just not the way he thought. "We can go out another time, for sure," I promised. I rushed to the back door and pulled it open. "Thanks, Billy! You're saving my life!"

He grinned and slipped through the door. I slammed it shut and let out a sigh of relief. "All clear," I said to Ashley, who was standing in the kitchen doorway.

"Mary-Kate, I don't think Billy understood what you were trying to tell him," she said. "You are heading for major danger!"

"I tried to explain!" I argued. "But I don't want to hurt his feelings. I'll just go on one little date with him—big deal. A quick soda and I'll never have to see him again!"

chapter six

"**E**xcellent party, Mom," I said later. "Everybody's having a great time."

Mom nodded as she arranged some shrimp on a big platter. "It's fun, isn't it, Mary-Kate? I can't wait for Jeanine and James to open all their gifts."

I popped a shrimp into my mouth. "I hope they like the Memory Book we got them."

"They'll love it." Mom handed me the platter. "By the way, where's Billy? I'm eager to meet him."

"He's on his way!" I said, escaping into the living room.

Uncle Brad turned from the photo collage. "Hey, there, Mary-Kate! How are you?" He took a shrimp and grinned at me. "I hear you have a new boyfriend."

"Uh . . . really?"

"Sure, your mother spread the word." He chuckled. "Where's the lucky guy?"

"Oh . . ." I gestured vaguely toward the front door. "He'll be here soon. Excuse me, Uncle Brad," I added quickly. "I'd better pass these around."

I hustled over to James, who was sitting on the couch. "Shrimp? Get 'em while they're cold!"

"Thanks, Mary-Kate." James had dark hair and a cute smile. He took a shrimp and eyed me over the top of his glasses. "Where's this Billy your mother's been talking about? He's on his way, I hope."

"Definitely," I lied.

"Good, I want to meet him. Make sure he's Mary-Kate–worthy," James teased.

I laughed and escaped with the shrimp again. But as I wandered around the living room and out onto the patio, everybody kept asking me about Billy.

"What did Mom do, rent space on a bill-board?" I complained to Ashley when I took the empty platter back into the kitchen. *"Coming Soon to a Theater Near You—Mary-Kate Has a New Boyfriend!"*

"Hmm, catchy title," Ashley said, taking a

bowl of fruit from the refrigerator. "Does it have a happy ending?"

"Very funny," I grumbled. "I keep telling everyone Billy will be here any second, but they won't stop asking about him."

"Yeah, Dad's watching out the front window," Ashley said, nodding toward the living room.

I groaned.

"Mary-Kate, why don't you just tell the truth?" Ashley suggested.

"Now?" I cried. "In the middle of the party?"

"Maybe not now, but as soon as the party's over. You'll have to fib one more time—pretend Billy called and said he isn't coming. Then, after the party, tell Mom and Dad the whole story."

I shook my head. "But if I can just get through tonight, nobody needs to know *any*thing!"

Aaron stuck his head in from the patio and smiled at Ashley. "Hey, are you coming back?"

"I'm on my way." Ashley grabbed the fruit bowl. "Just do it!" she whispered to me as she hurried to the door.

"No!" I shot back. I couldn't give up yet. But Ashley had given me an idea. If I pretended Billy called to say he wasn't coming, all I had to do was come up with a good excuse why.

My cell phone rang. I snatched it up from the kitchen desk.

"Hi, how's the party?" Brittany asked. "Have they opened their goodies yet?"

"Not yet," I said. I heard a lot of voices in the background. "Where are you?"

"At Click, with Lauren and Ben," Brittany said. "The place is jammed for Malcolm's Monster Movie Night."

"Oh, right!" Malcolm worked part-time at Click and organized a big movie festival every month. "Sounds wild."

"It's crazy! Whoa, they're dimming the lights," Brittany said. "Gotta go!"

I punched off and turned to see Mom coming through the doorway. "Was that Billy?" she asked.

"Umm . . . yeah," I murmured.

"Did he say when he'll get here?" she asked. "We're just about ready to open the gifts."

"He's not . . . ummm . . ." I started to panic.

"Mary-Kate, is everything all right?" Mom asked. "You look a little upset."

I was. But not the way she thought I was.

"Honey, what's the matter?" Mom looked worried.

"Billy can't make it," I told her.

"Oh, no," Mom said. "What happened? Is he all right?"

"Uh, yes, he's all right, but—"

"Is there a problem? Was there some kind of accident?" Mom set down the platter she was carrying and wiped her hands.

"Ummm, yes, an—an accident," I stammered. "On his way here."

Mom gasped. "Oh, no! Did they take him to the hospital?"

I nodded. She looked so horrified, I felt awful.

"It was a very minor accident," I assured her. "He fell off his bike, and he probably broke his arm, but he'll be okay!"

"Well, that's a relief," Mom said. "But, still, I know you're upset, Mary-Kate." She put her arm around my shoulders in a comforting squeeze.

Talk about guilt! I felt so bad I couldn't even speak.

"Listen, if you want to leave and go see him at the hospital, I'll explain everything," Mom told me.

"Leave the party? I don't—"

Stop right there, I told myself. Your amazing, incredible boyfriend is in the hospital! Mom will definitely smell a rat if you don't rush to his side.

"I don't want to disappoint Jeanine and James," I finished in a lame voice.

"Don't worry. They'll understand," she assured me. "Everyone will."

"Well . . . okay," I said reluctantly. "Thanks, Mom."

As she went into the living room, I took the car keys, my cell phone, and my purse and headed for the side door.

"Where are you going?" Ashley asked, coming in from the patio.

"I don't know yet," I said, grouchily explaining the situation.

"But it's almost time for the presents!" Ashley said.

"Don't remind me!" I pleaded as I went out the door. "I'm going to miss all the fun!"

"Mary-Kate, what are you doing here?" Lauren asked twenty minutes later. "Is the shower over? Why are you still dressed up?"

"I had to leave in a hurry," I said, sinking into the booth at Click. With everyone else wearing T-shirts and jeans, I felt a little ridiculous in my party dress. "It's a long story."

"We've got time," Brittany said. *"The Revenge*

of the Slime tape got jammed. So tell. And don't leave out any of the juicy details." She grinned at me.

I sighed and glanced around the crowded café. Malcolm and Ben, Lauren's boyfriend, were fiddling with the tape machine. Everyone else was scarfing down popcorn while they waited.

"Okay, here goes," I said.

I told them the whole story, starting with George and ending with "Billy's accident."

When I finished, Brittany shook her head. "Whoa. You are in deep."

"I know," I agreed. "I really messed up."

"What are you going to do?" Lauren asked.

"I'm not sure yet," I admitted, nibbling on some popcorn. "I can't say I broke up with Billy *now*. That would sound so cruel, when he was just in an accident."

Brittany rolled her eyes. "Reality check— there is no Billy, remember? Especially one with his arm in a cast."

"Hmm," I said. "I didn't say for sure he broke his arm though. If I find another Billy, I could say he just sprained it."

"But that means you'll have to take him to the wedding," Lauren pointed out.

I groaned. Could things get any *more* complicated?

"Mary-Kate!" a boy called.

I turned—and saw Will Foster waving at me from a back table.

Oh, yes. Things could definitely get more complicated.

"Oh, no, it's Billy!" I whispered, waving back. "I mean Will, the one I got rid of!"

Will hurried over to our table. "This is excellent!" he said, his brown eyes shining happily. "I never thought you'd ditch the party for me!"

"I . . . I . . ." I stammered. I couldn't think what to say!

"Come on over to my table," Will said. "Bring your friends. We can all sit together."

He looked so happy, I couldn't say no. "Come on, you guys," I said to Lauren and Brittany. *"Please!"* I begged.

We all threaded our way to Will's table, where three of his friends were sitting. I guess he really *had* bragged about me, because they acted impressed.

"They've been on my case all night," Will whispered as we sat down. "They didn't believe we really had a date."

Will put his arm around the back of my chair

and grinned proudly at his friends. I shot a panicky look at Lauren and Brittany.

Brittany rolled her eyes again, but she came to the rescue by talking about the monster movie.

"Have you guys seen *Revenge of the Slime* before?" she asked the boys. "The last scene is disgusting!"

I relaxed a little as they compared gross-out notes. Then I felt something brush against my fingers. I froze.

Was that Will's hand?

I hoped not. It had to be an accident, I told myself. He wouldn't try to hold my hand! Would he?

Will's fingers curled over mine.

He would.

A blaring car horn saved me. "Yikes, that was loud!" I cried, jerking my hand away from Will's.

One of the boys twisted around and peered out the front window. "It's my mom. We've got to go, guys."

Yes! I thought. *Thank you, Mrs. Whoever!*

"Bye, Mary-Kate," Will said, standing up to leave. "Listen, it's really cool that you came and . . ." He leaned close and lowered his voice. "I can't wait to see you again. Want to come hang out at my house Monday after school?"

"Well, but . . ." I sputtered. "I can't . . . I mean, I don't know where you live."

Brilliant, Mary-Kate.

"One twenty-three Fourth." Will grinned. "No way can you forget that one, right?"

"Hey, Foster, come on!" one of his friends shouted from the doorway.

"Bye, Mary-Kate. See you Monday after school, okay?" He ran out before I could stop him and say no. No, it was *not* okay.

"What just happened?" I asked Brittany and Lauren. "Do I have to go to his house on Monday?"

"I don't know," Lauren said. We stood up and went back to our table. "It kind of seems like he's expecting you."

"But I never said I would go!" I protested.

"Maybe you *should* go," Brittany said, "and explain this whole mess to him once and for all."

"Good idea," I said. I couldn't let Will think I liked him as a boyfriend. As soon as the wedding craziness was over, I'd tell him everything.

Ben and Malcolm joined us at our table.

"The machine ate the tape," Ben reported, putting his arm around Lauren. "It's ruined."

"I'll put on another one," Malcolm said. "How

about *I Dated a Mutant Zombie from Outer Space?*"

"Don't you have *I Dated a Freshman?*" I asked. "That's about the most horrible situation I can think of right now."

Ben and Malcolm looked confused.

"Is that supposed to be funny?" Malcolm asked.

"Mary-Kate's got a problem." Brittany explained it to them. We started to discuss it, when Malcolm's cell phone rang.

"Hey, Soph." It was Malcolm's girlfriend calling from her family vacation in Vancouver.

"No, it's a total disaster, as usual," Malcolm said. But it's not like the audience cares. I could show *Beach Blanket Bingo* and they'd never know the difference. Heh-heh." He laughed his half-snort half-laugh.

"Malcolm sure knows a lot about movies," I said to Brittany.

"He knows a lot about a lot of things," she said.

"And he's funny," Lauren added, "in his own weird way."

Brittany laughed. "Too bad his name isn't Billy."

Zing! My brain suddenly came alive.

"Who's to say his name *isn't* Billy?" I asked.

"I do," Ben said. "His name definitely isn't Billy."

"No—but he can *pretend* to be Billy!" I declared. "He's perfect! He doesn't know it yet, but he's my date for the wedding!"

chapter seven

"So after you left, they opened all their presents," I reported to Mary-Kate on Sunday morning. "They totally loved the Memory Book."

"That's great!" Mary-Kate poured syrup on her blueberry waffle. "What about the games? Did everybody play?"

I nodded. "Lainie and Alyssa and Diane wouldn't let anybody off the hook. We wrote MadLibs for the Future, and they were hilarious."

"It sounds like a blast," Mary-Kate said. "I still can't believe I missed out on the fun stuff."

You didn't have to miss out, I thought. But I bit my lip so I wouldn't say the words. I could see she felt bad about leaving the shower.

"In a way it was good that I left," Mary-Kate said, sipping orange juice. "If I hadn't gone to

Click, I might never have figured out what to do."

I looked up from my waffle. "What do you mean?"

Mary-Kate glanced around. "Where are Mom and Dad?" she whispered.

"Dad had to go to the office and Mom's out power-walking," I said. "Mary-Kate, don't tell me you have another plan!"

She grinned. "Don't worry, this one will definitely work. I have a new Billy."

My heart sank. "Oh, no," I said. "Who?"

"Malcolm!"

"Malcolm?" I groaned. "You're not seriously going to bring Malcolm to the wedding?"

I liked Malcolm a lot, but he wasn't exactly boyfriend material. He was funny in a sour way and very smart but down on everything and everyone, except for Sophie.

"Why not? He's perfect," Mary-Kate insisted. "He can talk about anything, whether he knows about it or not. And usually he knows all about everything, anyway. He probably knows more about debating, rock climbing, and acoustic guitar than anybody at the wedding will."

"But what about Sophie?" I protested. "Did Malcolm actually say he'd do this?"

"No," Mary-Kate admitted. "I haven't asked him yet. But Sophie's on vacation. She doesn't have to know anything about it. And I bet she'd understand if we explained it. What's the big deal? There's nothing between Malcolm and me."

"Mary-Kate, I smell another disaster!" I said.

"Shhh, here comes Mom!"

The back door opened and Mom stepped in, pink-cheeked and slightly out of breath. "Mary-Kate, there you are," she said. "I was asleep when you came in last night. What happened at the hospital? How's Billy?"

"He's, um, better," Mary-Kate replied, keeping her eyes on her plate. "He's home now. His arm wasn't broken after all. So no cast. Just a sling."

So Malcolm will be wearing a sling at the wedding, I thought as I took my plate to the dishwasher. *I hope Mary-Kate remembers to tell him about it.*

"Oh, that's good news." Mom filled a glass with water and took a drink. "Well, I guess Ashley's been telling you all about the shower."

Mary-Kate nodded. "I'm really sorry I couldn't get home sooner."

"We missed you." Mom finished her water and set the glass in the sink. "Were you at the hospital with Billy the whole time Mary-Kate?" she asked.

Alert! Alert! The trap-alarm went off in my brain. Mary-Kate couldn't see Mom's expression, but *I* could. Mom knew something!

I had to warn Mary-Kate that Mom was on to her. I "accidentally" slammed the dishwasher door so she'd look at me.

"Where else would I be?" Mary-Kate said.

Then she looked at me!

I gave a tiny shake of my head, but it was too late.

"That's a good question," Mom remarked. "When I was out walking with Phoebe just now, she told me her daughter went to Click last night for a monster movie festival."

"Oh." Mary-Kate's face flushed. "Really?"

I cringed. Mary-Kate was trapped, and she knew it!

"Really," Mom said. "And her daughter happened to mention that she saw *you* there."

Mary-Kate's flush deepened.

I had to help her out. "Mom, Click was probably dark because of the movies and—"

Mom shook her head at me. "Phoebe's daughter described your sister's dress," she said. "Mary-Kate, if you were supposed to be at the hospital with Billy, then what were you doing at Click?"

That's it, I thought helplessly. *There's no way Mary-Kate can lie her way out of this one!*

Thanks for trying, Ashley, I thought.

My mind went totally blank. Finally, after a few seconds, it started working again.

"I did go to Click," I admitted. "Um—for a brownie. For Billy. Mocha swirl. They're his favorite. He was feeling rotten, and I thought it would make him feel better."

I took a big bite of my waffle.

Mom laughed a little. "I knew there had to be a logical explanation! After all, it wouldn't be like you to hang out at Click while Billy's in the emergency room!"

"Mmm," I mumbled, still chewing. Close one.

"You know, I don't think you've ever told me Billy's last name," Mom said.

I gulped and pretended to choke.

"Lassiter," Ashley said, coming to my rescue. "Billy Lassiter."

"Right," I croaked. *Lassiter*, I thought. *I hope I remember it!*

"Your father and I can't wait to meet him." Mom smiled at me. "Why not invite him over for dinner tonight?"

"Tonight?" I almost choked for real. "Tonight's no good for Billy because . . ." I gulped my juice and tried to think. A debate? No, not on Sunday night. His arm's sprained, so he can't be playing guitar in a gig. "He's running that food drive, remember? He'll be busy until way past dinnertime."

"Oh, that's right. Well invite him over soon, though," Mom said.

"Definitely." I jumped up and took my plate to the dishwasher. I had to get out of there before I told any more lies. "See you later!"

"Where are you off to?"

Just one more little fib! "The community center!" I said as I raced out of the kitchen.

"Thanks, Aaron," I said over my cell phone. "I didn't know Mary-Kate was going to take the car. I absolutely have to get to Ava's on time."

"No problem," he told me. "I'll pick you up in twenty minutes."

Thank goodness my boyfriend was real, not

imaginary! I took a speedy shower, put on my pink robe, and opened my closet door.

Skirt and a top? I wondered. A top and pants? A dress?

I pulled out a couple of dresses. Nice, but not professional-looking. And most of my skirts were either too casual or too dressy.

I dug deeper into the closet and found a pair of mocha linen pants with a matching jacket. Simple and elegant. My lemon-colored top would look great with them. Where was it?

Laundry room. I ran downstairs and almost bumped into Mom. She was heading for the side door in the kitchen, carrying a full grocery bag in each arm.

"I'll get the door," I said, pulling it open. I peered into one of the bags as she passed by. "Hey, that's food from last night. What's going on?"

"We have so much left over!" Mom said over her shoulder. "There's not enough room in the refrigerator and it'll just go to waste. I decided to donate it to Billy's food drive."

"That's really . . . wait!" I cried, still in my bathrobe, trotting out to the car with her. "You mean you're taking it over to the community center? Now?"

"Of course. Why not?" she asked curiously.

Because there is *no food drive! There is no Billy!* I thought. Ha—if I didn't know it really existed, I wouldn't even believe there was a community center!

"Well, because . . ." I sputtered. But my brain blanked and I couldn't come up with a good excuse.

Mom loaded the sacks into the trunk with a bunch of others, then got into the car. The second she pulled out, Aaron pulled in.

I stared down at my bathrobe in a panic. I had to get dressed and go to Ava's office! But I also had to find Mary-Kate and warn her.

How was I going to do both?

chapter eight

"Mary-Kate, can you hear me?" I cried into my cell phone.

". . . don't . . . to . . ."—*crackle, crackle*—". . . me?"

My sister's voice faded in and out as Aaron drove me to Ava's. I called Mary-Kate's cell and found her at Click, but both our phones got terrible reception there.

"Emergency, Mary-Kate!" I shouted. "Mom's on her way to the community center!"

Crackle, crackle. " . . . you later and . . ." More crackling. Then the connection totally broke up.

"She couldn't hear me!" I said to Aaron, punching off in frustration. "She doesn't have a clue what's coming! What am I going to do?"

Aaron stopped for a red light. "Try her when

you get to Ava's. Call Click's office phone—somebody will get her for you."

"By then it'll be too late." I glanced around the intersection. "Get in the right lane."

"Huh? Why?" Aaron pointed straight ahead. "Beverly Hills is that way."

"Right, but the community center is that way," I told him, pointing right. "We can get there fast if we use the back roads. And we'll still be able to get to Ava's in time!"

"I get it—we're going to intercept your mom," Aaron said, easing into the right lane. "Got a story for her?"

"Not yet," I admitted. "I'll try to think of something on the way. Too bad I can't reach Mary-Kate—she's the one who's so good at making up stories!"

With the back roads almost empty, Aaron and I got to the community center without a problem. Mom's car was already in the parking lot near the white stucco building, but she was just climbing out. We'd made it!

"Hi, Mrs. Olsen!" Aaron called out the window.

"Well, Aaron, hi," Mom said, surprised. "What are you two doing here? Ashley, aren't you supposed to be at Ava's?"

"Uh, yes." I got out of the car. "But see, Mary-Kate called me. They're on their way to the shelter now."

"Billy's not trying to drive, I hope." Mom frowned.

Why not? I wondered in a panic.

"Not with that arm," Mom added.

Oh, the arm! Broken? Sprained? I couldn't keep things straight! "I don't think he's driving, Mom," I said. "Anyway, Aaron and I will take the food for you."

"But what about your meeting?" she asked.

"*After* the meeting," Aaron chimed in. "First we go to Ava's, *then* the shelter."

I shot him a thank-you glance. It made crazy sense to me, but Mom looked confused. "I still don't understand why I shouldn't leave the food here," she said. "Wouldn't it be quicker for Mary-Kate or someone else to come pick it up?"

I couldn't let her talk to anybody in the center about a food drive that didn't exist!

"No, because everybody's staying at the shelter to help give out the food," I told her. I couldn't believe how fast I was coming up with the lies.

Aaron got out of his car and opened the hatchback. "Let's load up, Mrs. O!"

• • •

With three minutes to spare before the meeting, I kissed Aaron on the cheek and hopped out of his car. As I pulled open the glass door to Ava's building, I caught sight of my reflection in the glass door.

Wrinkled pants, hair starting to frizz from the heat . . . and was that a stain on my yellow top? I got into the elevator and took a closer look. Definitely a stain. I quickly buttoned my jacket. Why had I carried the teriyaki chicken?

The elevator stopped and I got off. No one was in the reception area, which had sleek modern furniture, a silk rug, and bowls of flowers on low glass tables. Photos of celebrities hung on the walls.

Imagine having a summer job in a place like this! I thought.

"Hi, Ashley. Good, you're on time," Ava said crisply. She walked out of her private office carrying a few sheets of paper. She looked cool and elegant as usual, in a slim skirt and silk blouse.

"Would you like a croissant?" she offered, gesturing to a china plate on the reception desk. "A new bakery just opened on Melrose. They're fabulous."

"No, thank you," I told her. I couldn't sit

around and eat croissants while Aaron waited out in his car. "I had a big breakfast."

"Okay, here's what I need," Ava said, handing me the papers. "Jeanine revised her seating plan and you need to deliver the list to Tina-Ming Su. She's the calligrapher who's doing the place cards."

"No problem," I told her. "Just tell me where."

"Her studio's in Pacific Palisades," Ava said, handing me a computer printout of a map with an address clipped to it. "She's incredibly talented, so she's always booked solid. I was lucky to get her for Jeanine. The thing is, while she's working, she doesn't answer her phone."

"I guess she has to concentrate," I said.

Ava nodded. "She's due to start working on Jeanine's place cards at noon. And I haven't been able to tell her about the new list. You have to get it to her in time."

I took a quick peek at my watch. *Yikes, it was a little after eleven!* "No problem!" I repeated.

I raced out of the office and back to the car. "Pacific Palisades, and step on it!" I half joked.

"What about all the food?" Aaron asked as he pulled away from the curb. "My car is starting to stink."

I sniffed. The combination of chicken and garlic and fruit and shrimp *was* pretty awful. Plus the day was getting hotter. A lot of the stuff was going to spoil.

But Mom thought we'd be giving it to the homeless. I couldn't dump it.

"I know another shelter!" I said. "We raised money for it in seventh grade and they invited us to visit. It's not too far from here." I checked out the map Ava gave me.

"What about the calligrapher?" Aaron asked.

"The shelter's on the way," I replied, checking my watch. "I'm positive we can make it!"

chapter nine

"So you'll do it?" I asked Malcolm. His shift was over and we were sitting in a booth at Click. "You'll play Billy?"

"What's in it for me?" Malcolm asked.

"When it's over, I'll give you an Oscar," I joked.

He shook his head. "Sorry. Not good enough."

I racked my brain, trying to think of something I had that Malcolm might want. "What if I take over your shift here at Click?" I offered. "For a week. You get the paycheck, I do the work."

He nodded. "Deal."

"Thanks, Malcolm." I wasn't looking forward to a week of volunteering at Click, but if this worked out, it would be worth it. "But what about Sophie? You're sure she won't mind?"

"I don't think so," he said. "I'll explain it to her

when she gets back. She'll probably think it's funny."

"Great. Oh, there's something you have to wear, sort of a costume," I added.

I unzipped my backpack and pulled out a sling. I'd bought it on the way to Click. "Billy has a sprained arm," I explained.

"I have to wear this the whole time?" Malcolm slipped the sling over his shoulder and around his arm. "Why can't Billy wear an eye patch? I always wanted to wear an eye patch."

"Maybe next time," I said. "You sprained your arm falling off your bike, by the way. You were coming to my house for the bridal shower."

"So Billy's a klutz," Malcolm said. "Anything else I should know?"

"A lot, actually," I said. "Want to go to the mall? We can practice being a couple there, and I'll fill you in. Plus, I'm dying for a lemon frozen yogurt."

Malcolm frowned. "I hate the mall. It gives me a headache."

"Come on, Malcolm," I pleaded. "We can go see that new movie, *The Gorgon*."

He made a face. "Please. It's a remake—and it stinks compared to the Japanese original. But I've seen it only three times. . . ."

We wandered around the mall for half an hour, waiting for the movie to start. I told him everything he needed to know about Billy. He memorized it easily.

"You're a genius!" I told him. "If only I'd asked you to be Billy in the first place!"

"Yeah. I could be wearing an eye patch instead of *this*." Malcolm held up his "sprained" arm.

"Yeah, but look at all the sympathy you're getting because of the sling! See?" I pointed to two girls from school—Trish and Maryann—who were watching us from across the food court.

"They aren't sympathetic, they're nosy," Malcolm declared. "I bet they're wondering what we're doing together."

"I bet you're right." I laughed. "They probably think we're a couple!"

Good, I thought. If we could fool kids from school, we could definitely fool my parents.

We turned the corner. Dozens of people had already lined up to see *The Gorgon*.

"We'd better get in line," Malcolm said. "I don't want to sit in the front row."

He grabbed my hand and pulled me to the line. It was already at least forty people long. I spotted Joanne and Zach up ahead and waved.

After a few seconds, I realized that Malcolm was still holding my hand. I glanced at him. "This feels weird," I said.

Malcolm dropped my hand. "You're telling me. Face it, Mary-Kate, we're just not meant for each other."

"Yeah, but we *look* like we are." I nodded at our reflections in a store window. Malcolm's not the cutest guy in school, but he has his own kind of charm. We didn't look bad together. There was zero attraction between us—but you couldn't tell by looking at us.

And Ashley said this was a bad idea, I thought. Is *she* in for a major surprise!

This is working out perfectly!

Aaron gripped the steering wheel and squinted at the street sign ahead. "Coriander Way?"

"Coriander *Street*," I said, anxiously checking the map again.

"This place is a maze," Aaron muttered, slowly driving forward.

"I know, I'm sorry," I apologized. "We must be

getting close!" According to my map, it had to be around here somewhere.

I couldn't blame Aaron for being grumpy. I felt the same way. The air conditioner was on the blink and we were both sweating. And even with the windows open, the food fumes kept getting stronger.

I looked at my watch. Eleven-twenty and we hadn't even found the shelter yet!

"Check it out, Ashley!" Aaron pointed to another street sign. "Am I seeing things, or is that Coriander Street?"

"It is! We're going to make it!" I laughed with relief as he turned the corner.

Aaron pulled to a stop in front of the shelter. As he started unloading the bags of food, I went to find someone in charge of taking donations.

The front door was locked. I banged on it. No one came. As I turned away, I noticed the handwritten sign under my foot.

USE THE SIDE DOOR, PLEASE.

I raced around the corner. Wrong side! I ran back around to the other side and burst through the door. "I have a donation of food!" I said breathlessly to a man sitting at a desk. "Should I bring it in here?"

He smiled and shook his head. "The back

door goes right into the kitchen," he said. "Leave it with Dory or Mike. They'll take care of it. And thanks a lot."

"You're welcome!" I called over my shoulder. I sped back to the car and grabbed two bags of food. "Follow me!" I told Aaron.

A few minutes later, all the food was finally delivered. "It's twenty to twelve!" Aaron called as we raced back to the car. "How far away is the calligrapher?"

"Only a few blocks." I threw myself inside and buckled my seat belt.

Aaron grinned. Pumping the gas, he turned the key. The engine started, then stalled. Aaron tried again, but the engine didn't catch at all. "I don't believe this," he muttered. "I flooded it. We have to wait for it to clear."

I peeked at my watch—and really panicked. It was almost noon! I couldn't wait!

chapter ten

I grabbed my cell phone and punched in Mary-Kate's number. Luckily, this time her phone worked.

"Major emergency!" I declared as soon as she answered. "Drop everything and come pick me up!"

"I'm on my way!" she replied. "Wait—where to?"

I gave her the address of the shelter.

"Okay, I'm going down the escalator now," she reported.

"What escalator? Where *are* you?"

"At the mall with Malcolm," she said. "We were going to see a movie, but it's sold out. Ashley, what's wrong?"

The mall! I thought she'd be home by now!

"I'll explain everything later. Just get here as fast as you can!"

I punched off and turned to Aaron. "She's just leaving the mall!"

He checked the time. "It's gonna be close, but if the lights are with her, she might make it."

Aaron cupped his hand around the back of my neck and gave it a gentle squeeze. But I was way too stressed to relax. I was hot, I smelled of garlic and shrimp, my outfit was totally wrinkled—and I might not get to the calligrapher's in time.

And it was Mary-Kate's fault!

"There she is!" Aaron declared after what seemed like an hour. "I'll stay here and wait for the engine to clear. Good luck!"

I leaned across the seat and gave him a quick kiss. "Thanks for everything, Aaron. Call you later!"

I ran to our car and jumped in next to Mary-Kate. As she pulled away, I forced myself to look at my watch. "We're never going to make it!"

"Make it where?" Mary-Kate asked. She sniffed the air. "What's that smell?"

"Eau de shrimp," I snapped. "Plus bleu cheese, garlic, and a touch of teriyaki to spice it up."

"Ashley, would you please tell me what's going on?"

"A disaster, that's what!" I said. I gave her directions to the calligrapher's. Then I explained the situation, starting with Mom's idea to take the leftover shower food to the shelter.

"Aaron and I finally found another shelter, but then his engine flooded," I finished. "That's when I called you."

"Wow, Ashley, you saved me from major trouble!" Mary-Kate exclaimed. "You're totally the best!"

"Yeah, but now *I'm* in trouble," I declared. "It's one minute to noon now. I'm going to be late."

"Maybe not. The calligrapher's clock could be slow," Mary-Kate suggested hopefully.

"Not slow enough," I said. "This assignment was really important, Mary-Kate, and I've messed it up!"

"Thanks to me, you mean," she said in a small voice.

I nodded. I was angry and I couldn't hide it. I didn't *want* to hide it. Her little white lies had gotten *me* into trouble!

My cell phone rang. I checked the caller I.D. "Oh, no!"

"Who is it?"

"Ava." As I stared at the phone, it rang again. No way did I want to talk to her. But I had to. "Hello?"

"Ashley, hello. Tell me you got the list to the calligrapher's in time," Ava said.

"I didn't get it there in time," I confessed.

"Oh, no, why not? Ashley, this was extremely important!" Ava cried. "What happened?"

I hesitated. I *could* make up some kind of story—there was a huge traffic jam, my watch battery died—but I decided not to. Nothing I said would make Ava happy, so I might as well tell the truth.

"I had to do another errand first," I explained. "I thought I had plenty of time, but then the car broke down. I'm almost at the calligrapher's now, but I'm late. I'm sorry, Ava."

"What a mess!" Ava declared. "Okay, give the list to Tina-Ming Su anyway. And then . . . Ashley, that'll be it. Thanks for your work so far, but I really don't think this is your kind of job."

"Was she angry?" Mary-Kate asked as I hung up.

I nodded.

"How angry?"

I stared at her, hard. "Angry enough to fire me!"

Later, I sprawled on Ashley's bed and waited for her to finish talking to Jeanine.

"I'm really sorry, Jeanine," Ashley said. "By the time we got there, Tina-Ming Su had already started on your list."

While she listened to Jeanine, Ashley ran a comb through her wet hair. The first thing she did when we got home was dump her smelly, wrinkled clothes and take a long, hot shower.

"But it *does* matter," Ashley said into the phone. "I know you have to pay extra for any changes."

I guiltily nibbled a fingernail. This whole thing was my fault!

Ashley smiled a little. "That's really great of you to say, Jeanine. Thanks for understanding. But I'm still sorry. Okay . . . yes. Bye."

"So Jeanine's okay with everything?" I asked.

"She's not mad, if that's what you mean," Ashley replied. "It's not like I goofed up on purpose."

"Right!" I agreed. "Why couldn't Ava be like that?"

Ashley shot me a look. "Ava's not our cousin. She's my boss. Make that *was* my boss. There's no chance I'll be her summer assistant now."

"Don't give up yet!" I said, scooting off the bed. "The job is totally perfect for you. I'll help you think of a way to get back in with her!"

"How?"

"I don't know yet, but I'll think of something," I promised. "You deserve it, after everything that's happened. The way you covered for me with Mom was so great. You saved my life!"

"Thanks. But, Mary-Kate? Promise not to come up with any more white lies about anything," Ashley warned. "All they do is cause trouble."

"Not all of them," I pointed out. "You lied to Lainie, remember? You told her she looked great in the bridesmaid dress. And you know she didn't!"

"That was a totally different kind of lie!" Ashley said. "It made Lainie feel better. And that's all. It wasn't some complicated plot!"

"It got complicated only because of Will!" I argued. "But now that I've got Malcolm, everything's under control. And the wedding is in six days. After that, no more lies." I held up one hand. "Promise!"

chapter eleven

"Only two more days until the wedding," I said to Malcolm at the mall on Thursday. I'd called him to ask for extra rehearsal time. "Are you nervous?"

"No," Malcolm said. "This isn't exactly Shakespeare, you know."

"Maybe not," I said. "But it's not that easy for me." We practiced holding hands. It felt strange, but I slowly started getting used to it. *By Saturday, we should have this couple thing down perfectly*, I thought.

"How are you coming on your areas of expertise, Billy?" I asked, trying out his stage name.

"Well, I already know something about debating," Malcolm said. "Who doesn't. And acoustic guitar isn't exactly an exotic subject. But rock climbing . . . well, I know something about the geology of rocks. But as a sport I think it's pretty stupid."

"Just pretend to like it," I said, checking out his muscles—what there were of them—through his T-shirt. He didn't really look like the rock-climber type, if you know what I mean. But it was too late to worry about that.

"No problem, honeybunch," he said. "Light of my life, apple of my eye, center of my universe, Juliet to my Romeo . . ."

"That's enough, Billy," I said. I waved to a couple of girls from school as we kept walking. "This wedding is getting pretty crazy. There's so much to do! That wedding planner made a huge mistake when she fired Ashley."

Malcolm nodded. I'd already told him about Sunday's disaster. "Yeah. Firing Ashley is always a mistake," he said.

"I'm trying to figure out how to get Ava to give her another chance," I said. "But I have a feeling Ashley doesn't want me to."

"Why not?" he asked. "You said she loved the job."

"She's afraid I'll make things worse," I admitted.

"No! Not you!" Malcolm said. "Your life is

completely under control. And my name is Billy."

"Ha-ha." I punched him softly in the arm. "Hey, where's your sling?"

"Oh, yeah, I forgot." Malcolm took the sling from his backpack and put it on. "Now I'm in character. Billy's so *complex*."

We walked on, then stopped at a smoothie stand. As I dug into my backpack for some money, I found a folded piece of paper with my name written on it.

"Oh, no," I murmured. "Is this what I think it is?"

"What?" Malcolm asked.

I unfolded the note and read it to myself.

Dear Mary-Kate,

Did I tell you how cool it was seeing you at Click? It'll be even cooler when you to come over to my house. I guess you're really busy, huh? Anyway, I can't wait to be together again, can you?

Will

"What is it?" Malcolm asked again.

"It's a note from Will Foster," I explained. I put the note in my backpack. "He was the first Billy."

"Oh, right. The freshman. Another smashing success for Ashley's famous Love Link." Malcolm wasn't a big fan of Ashley's matchmaking Website.

"He's put three notes in my locker this week," I sighed. "Somehow he got the crazy idea that I like him. As a boyfriend, I mean."

"Gee, how'd that happen?" Malcolm said, sticking a straw into his drink. "All you did was ask him out."

"I tried to explain it to him," I insisted. "But he won't listen! I feel terrible about it."

"Yeah, it's a real shame," Malcolm said.

He was kidding, but behind his sarcasm, he was right. It wasn't fair to just avoid Will. The longer I let him live in fantasyland, the worse he'd feel when he found out the truth.

"I'll tell him again," I promised, taking a sip of my strawberry smoothie. "As soon as I think of a nice way to say it."

"Good luck with that," Malcolm muttered. He stared across the corridor. "Mary-Kate, I think those people are waving at you." He pointed toward the Blue Ocean Grill.

I looked at the man and woman standing near the restaurant entrance—and panicked.

It was Mom and Dad!

I pasted a big smile on my face and waved back.

"Parent alert!" I muttered to Malcolm out of the corner of my mouth. "And they've seen us! What are we going to do?"

"Well, running would look a little suspicious," he said.

"This isn't funny!" I told him. "Oh, no! They're coming over here!"

"Time for my big debut," Malcolm said. "Relax, Mary-Kate. Everything's cool."

My heart thumped. A zillion butterflies floated around my stomach. How could I possibly relax when everything could suddenly fall apart?

"Hi, honey!" Mom and Dad said as they walked up.

"Hi . . ." I swallowed. "What are you two doing here?"

"We decided to have an early dinner at the Blue Ocean Grill," Mom explained. She gave Malcolm a curious, friendly smile.

Malcolm jumped right in. "Hey, Mr. and Mrs. Olsen," he said, shaking their hands. "I'm Billy Lassiter. It's a *thrill* to meet you."

"And it's nice to meet *you!*" Mom replied. "Mary-Kate's told us so much about you."

Uh-oh, here come the questions about debating and rock climbing, I thought nervously. Did Malcolm know enough to fool them?

"She's told me a lot about you, too," Malcolm said, putting his arm around my shoulders.

"Uh-oh." Dad chuckled.

"Don't worry," Malcolm said. "Your secrets are safe with me."

Dad laughed a little uncomfortably.

Ooh, the way Malcolm turned that around on them was really smooth, I thought. I leaned against his side and relaxed a tiny bit.

"I'm sorry about your bike accident," Mom said. "How is your arm?"

"The pain was horrible," Malcolm replied, clutching his arm. "Horrible! Like a thousand burning needles stabbing into my bones! But it's better now. Thanks for asking."

"You probably miss playing the guitar," Dad said.

I tensed up again.

"Oh, yes," Malcolm agreed. "But it gives me a chance to really listen, you know? Did you ever really *listen* to music?"

"Um, I think so," Dad said. "I'm in the business."

"Right, the music biz," Malcolm said. "I guess you take musicians like me and chew them up and spit them out like so much—"

I grabbed Malcolm's free arm. "That's enough, Billy," I warned. He was getting a little carried away.

"You look familiar," Dad said, studying Malcolm's face. "Are you sure we haven't met?"

I thought fast. "You've probably seen him coming out of Click," I said. "You know, when you used to drop me off there."

"Yeah, I'm there all the time," Malcolm added.

"That must be it," Dad agreed. "So, Billy, Mary-Kate tells us you're a rock climber. Where do you like to go climbing?"

Malcolm jumped in again, naming rock formations and talking about different kinds of climbing gear. For all I knew, he was making it up. But it sounded good. Dad looked interested and Mom beamed at him.

I couldn't believe how well this was going! Another couple of minutes and Mom and Dad would go to dinner. It would be over!

Smiling, I relaxed against Malcolm's side. He kept his arm over my shoulder. We almost felt like a real couple.

Then I glanced around.

And froze.

Sophie, Malcolm's girlfriend, was standing by the candle store. Staring at us!

She's supposed to be on vacation! I thought. *What's she doing back so early?*

She looked totally shocked. I didn't blame her. There I was, standing extremely close to her boyfriend. And he had his arm around me!

We looked like a couple to everyone in the mall—including Sophie!

I nudged Malcolm, but he didn't notice. I wanted to warn him, but how could I do it without explaining the whole story to Mom and Dad?

It was too late, anyway. Sophie was storming toward us. Her red hair swung from side to side and her face was pink. She was totally furious—and hurt.

"I don't believe this!" she cried when she almost reached us. "People said it was true, but I didn't believe it!"

"Sophie?" Malcolm tensed up and dropped his arm from my shoulder. "What are you doing here?"

"We decided to . . . oh, never mind!" Sophie shouted. "What do you care if I'm back? It's obvious you don't care about me at all!"

Malcolm glanced at me. Then at Mom and Dad, who looked stunned. "Sophie, this isn't . . . I mean, Mary-Kate and I were—"

Malcolm and I were both trapped. How could we tell Sophie the truth with Mom and Dad standing right there?

"I know all about you and Mary-Kate!" Sophie snapped. "Terry and Marcia and a bunch of others told me."

Malcolm tried again. "Sophie, we're—"

"Forget it! Just forget it!" Sophie cried. She spun around and stalked away.

"Sophie, wait up!" Malcolm called. He gave me a panicked glance and ran after her.

Dad frowned at me in confusion. "What was that all about? Who was that girl?"

"It's . . ." I thought fast. One more little white lie, I decided. Just one more!

"That was Sophie," I replied. "She's, um, Billy's ex-girlfriend. He broke up with her a few weeks ago, but she's having problems with it. Obviously."

Mom shook her head sympathetically. "Poor girl. I suppose it hurt to see Billy with someone else."

I felt as bad as Mom. Worse. Because I felt horribly guilty, too. Thanks to me, Sophie thought Malcolm was cheating on her!

She was so mad and so hurt, I thought. I had to help Malcolm explain this!

"I'd better go catch him," I said. "Have a good dinner, you guys."

I raced off. I found Malcolm and Sophie on one side of the big fountain at the mall entrance.

Sophie hurried toward the door. Malcolm was walking backward in front of her, trying to get her to stop. Sophie shook her head and zigzagged around him.

"Sophie!" I called out.

She spun around. I could see she was crying.

"Go away, Mary-Kate!" she shouted. "Don't come after me or talk to me anymore! I trusted you! And now you've ruined everything!"

chapter twelve

Tomorrow's the big day! I thought as I went to my locker after school on Friday. Or, rather, the big *night*. By eight o'clock tomorrow, Jeanine and James will be married!

I still felt a little sad whenever I thought of Ava. But I tried not to think about it—the wedding was the most important thing.

I opened my locker and pulled a couple of books off the shelf. As I slid them into my backpack, my cell phone rang.

"Hello, is this Ashley Olsen?" a woman's voice asked.

"Yes?"

"Ashley, this is Tina-Ming Su. You gave me your number when you were at my studio on Sunday."

The calligrapher? Why was she calling *me*? "Yes?" I said again.

"I'm afraid I have a bit of a problem," Tina-Ming said. "I can't get in touch with Ava and I need to talk to her about Jeanine's place cards."

"Well . . ." I started to tell her I didn't work for Ava anymore. But I decided not to. Maybe I could do something. After all, this was my cousin's wedding. "I'll be glad to help if I can," I said.

"Jeanine changed the seating again, and Ava gave me several more place cards to redo yesterday," Tina-Ming explained. "She said she'd send someone to pick them up tonight. The problem is that my sister and I are going to a family reunion and we're leaving earlier than I planned."

"Oh, so you won't be at your studio," I said.

"That's right. And I don't want to leave them on the porch because it's raining," Tina-Ming said. "I'd like someone to come pick them up before I leave so I know they're safe."

"Got it. I'll try to find Ava and call you right back," I said.

I hung up and punched in Ava's number. It rang twice, then the answering machine picked up.

Maybe Jeanine knows where Ava is, I thought. I quickly called her house and got her father.

"Jeanine and her mother and Ava all went off to some fancy spa, Ashley," Uncle Scott reported. "They're getting massages and manicures—the works. Supposed to get rid of the pre-wedding jitters."

"Do you have the number?" I asked.

He gave it to me. "Is something wrong?"

Not yet, I thought. "No, don't worry, Uncle Scott," I said. "See you tomorrow!"

I called the spa and asked for Ava. They put me on hold.

While I was listening to New Age music, Aaron came up. I closed my locker and we headed for the door. The New Age music kept playing in my ear as I told him what happened.

"What's Ava supposed to do, jump out of the sauna and race to the calligrapher's?" he asked.

"No, she'll probably call somebody to go get the place cards," I said.

Finally, the music stopped. I waited, but no one came on the line. "Hello? Hello?"

I turned the phone off. "This is crazy. Why should I call Ava when I'm right here?"

"Because it's Ava's job?" Aaron suggested.

"But it's *my* cousin's wedding!" I declared. "And I'm going to help!"

96

• • •

Mary-Kate had the car, so I had to ask Aaron to drive me again! I called Tina-Ming Su and told her I was on my way.

"There's the shelter," I said to Aaron as we drove by. "I hope they liked the food."

"Want to stop and ask?" Aaron teased. "I promise not to flood the engine."

I giggled. "Thanks, but let's not take any chances!"

We drove past the shelter and took a winding road into Pacific Palisades. Tina-Ming Su's house was on a cul-de-sac. We stopped behind a silver Mini and I hopped out.

"Be right back!" I said. Pulling my blue hoodie up, I ran through the rain and trotted up the porch steps.

The door opened before I could knock. Tina-Ming Su stepped out with another woman and pulled the door shut.

"Hello, Ashley," she said. "This is my sister, Geri. Thank you for getting here so fast."

"No problem," I told her. Not this time, at least.

"Geri and I are in a bit of a hurry," Tina-Ming added. "We want to stop and get some croissants to take to the reunion. The bakery's on Melrose—Ava was raving about it to me—but it's a little out of the way."

Tina-Ming handed me a bundle of small white cards wrapped in plastic. "Here they are. The last of them, I hope."

"It better be!" I laughed. "The wedding's tomorrow."

"I'm sure it will be wonderful." Tina-Ming pulled a collapsible umbrella out of her bag. "Now we can be on our way. Thank you again, Ashley. Good luck at the wedding!"

Tina-Ming and her sister hurried to the Mini and drove off as I climbed in next to Aaron. "Got 'em!" I declared, showing him the cards.

"All right!" Aaron swung back onto the road. "Mission accomplished!"

"Almost," I said. "First I have to take them to Ava's office. *Then* it'll be over. How about some curly fries afterward? My treat."

"You're on."

As Aaron drove back toward town, I couldn't resist looking at the cards. I checked my hands to make sure they were clean enough, then unwrapped the plastic.

"No wonder everybody wants Tina-Ming Su to

do their calligraphy. It's really beautiful," I said admiringly.

I checked out another card—and gasped. I couldn't believe what I was seeing!

"What?" Aaron asked.

"Oh, no!" I cried, frantically turning up more cards. "She spelled James's family's last name wrong—six times! It's *Greene*! She left the *e* off the end!"

"Whoa," Aaron said. "Could somebody else add it?"

"No way. The spacing would be totally ruined." I shook my head. Jeanine would be really upset. So would James and his family—after all, it was *their* name!

And when Ava found out what happened, she'd blame me!

Friday after school, Malcolm and I were hanging out at his house, talking about Sophie.

"She won't listen to me, Mary-Kate," Malcolm said, slumping on the couch in his living room. "I called her a zillion times last night. Her mom finally told me to stop."

ul, seeing Malcolm so sad and how much he cared about Sophie.

guess she wouldn't speak to you today ol, either," I said, patting Malcolm on the ar

"Actually, she *did*." He sighed. "She said a bunch of kids told her they saw you and me hanging out at the mall together. They said we were acting all, you know, lovey-dovey."

I nodded, biting my lip guiltily. We *were* acting, but nobody else knew that! No wonder Sophie believed them.

"I tried to talk to her today, too, but she shut me out," I said. "She doesn't want to hear one word from me."

"Or me," Malcolm said softly. "I don't want to lose her, Mary-Kate. I don't know what to do."

I hunched my shoulders and stared at the carpet, feeling incredibly guilty. I never thought a couple of little white lies could cause so much trouble, but they did! Ashley lost her chance with Ava. Will thought I had a crush on him. I've been lying to my parents. And Malcolm and Sophie might break up!

It was my fault. I had to try to make things right.

"I'm calling her," I declared. I sat up, grabbed my purse, and pulled out my cell phone and punched in Sophie's number.

Malcolm straightened up and watched tensely.

"Sophie? It's me, Mary-Kate, don't hang—"

Sophie slammed the phone down.

"Up," I said to the dial tone.

chapter thirteen

I bundled up the place cards and nervously tapped my fingers on the plastic wrapping. As Aaron drove down the winding road out of the hills, I tried to come up with a plan.

"Do you still want to go to Ava's office?" Aaron asked, pulling up to a red light.

I shook my head. "I can't just drop a bunch of misspelled cards off. Ava will freak when she finds out."

"Yeah, but *you* didn't get the last name wrong," Aaron reminded me.

"I know, but I should have checked them before Tina-Ming left. Anyway, Ava's not the main problem," I added. "It's Jeanine and James's wedding. I want things to be perfect for them."

I gazed down at the cards as Aaron drove on.

Somehow, I had to get them fixed. And I knew only one person who could do it right.

Tina-Ming Su.

It might be too late, but I had to try it. "We have to catch up with Tina-Ming!" I exclaimed. "Quick, get on Melrose!"

"Melrose?" Aaron frowned. "You said she was going out of town."

"She is, but she's going to a bakery first!" I told him. "And she and her sister left the house only a few minutes ago. How far could they have gotten?"

"Let's check it out," Aaron agreed, shifting lanes. "I guess this means no curly fries, huh?"

I grinned. "Not yet. But how does a croissant sound?"

Aaron laughed and turned onto Melrose. The street went on forever, and the sidewalks were filled with shoppers.

I crossed my fingers and shifted my gaze from one side of the street to the other. *Please let me find her!* I thought.

She was wearing a raincoat. *Beige*, I thought. And her sister's umbrella? Red. No . . .

"Orange!" I cried. I pointed through the windshield at a bobbing neon-orange umbrella way up

ahead. "See that umbrella? That's them, I'm positive!"

"All right!" Aaron said, slowing down. "Let me
try to pull around this truck and—"

"Running's faster!" I shoved the cards into my
backpack and pushed open the door. "Thanks,
Aaron! I'll find you later!"

I jumped out of the car and leaped onto the
crowded sidewalk. I barreled along as fast as I
could, dodging shoppers and calling out "Excuse
me!" every two seconds.

My backpack thumped against my back and
my hood slid off. Rainwater trickled down my neck
and into my eyes, but I didn't dare slow down.

I had to keep that orange umbrella in sight!

The DON'T WALK sign started flashing up ahead.
I put on a burst of speed and raced across the
street just in time.

The umbrella was still up ahead. And now I
could see the back of a beige raincoat.

"Tina-Ming Su!" I shouted. "Tina-Ming Su!"

The umbrella kept bobbing along.

"Tina-Ming Su!" I shouted again. "Wait!
Please!" I dodged a group of women and their kids
and pounded down the sidewalk, gasping and
shouting.

Finally, finally, the umbrella stopped moving.

"Ashley?" Tina-Ming's eyes widened in surprise. "What on earth?"

"I *knew* I heard someone calling your name," her sister told her.

I gasped and tried to smile. Tina-Ming was carrying a white bakery box tied with thin red string. They'd already bought their croissants. Two more minutes and they would have hit the highway!

"I hate to bother you," I gasped. "But we have a problem!"

After I explained, Tina-Ming insisted on fixing the place cards that very instant. She had her ink and pens in the car, because she had some other work to do over the weekend.

The three of us went into the bakery and cleared off a back table. Her sister ate a croissant while Tina-Ming quickly added *e*'s to the six place cards.

"I can work fast if I have to," she said with a wink.

I don't know how she did it! The *e*'s looked as if they'd always been there.

"These are perfect," I told her as we left the bakery. "Thank you!"

"Not a problem," she said. "I'm glad you caught me so I could fix them."

We said good-bye and they headed for their car. I started back down the sidewalk, looking for Aaron. After a couple of minutes, I suddenly remembered—I'd promised him a croissant.

He definitely deserved it!

As I hurried back to the bakery, my cell phone rang.

"Ashley!" Ava's voice said. "Tell me you have the place cards!"

"I have the place cards," I said. "How did you know?"

"I just called Tina-Ming Su—she left a message earlier, but I didn't get it until now," Ava explained. "She told me the whole story. It sounds like you have things under control."

I smiled to myself. I *did* have things under control!

"The cards are perfect now," I said. "I'm going to take them to your office in a few minutes."

"You definitely nipped that disaster in the bud," Ava said. "Good work, Ashley. I'm impressed at the way you handled it. And I'm thinking I was wrong the other day."

"What do you mean?" I asked, tucking a wet

strand of hair behind my ear. Could she mean . . .

"I was a little too quick to judge you," Ava admitted. "You might make a mistake here and there. But you think fast and you can handle a crisis. That's the kind of assistant I need. So, if you like, you can come work for me anytime."

If I like? I thought, grinning happily at all the shoppers flowing around me. "I would *love* it!" I exclaimed.

On Saturday morning, Ashley and I put on our bridesmaid dresses and modeled them for Lauren and Brittany. They'd slept over Friday and we'd promised them a sneak preview.

"How do we look?" I asked as my sister and I paraded around my bedroom in our long blue dresses.

"Totally fabulous," Brittany declared, sitting cross-legged on the bed. "I love that color."

"Me, too. Hey, are those new necklaces?" Lauren asked.

Ashley nodded and fingered the gold chain with its small rose pendant enameled in pink. "Jeanine gave one to each of the bridesmaids."

"Was that my phone?" I suddenly asked.

"I didn't hear anything," Lauren said.

I grabbed my backpack off the floor and dumped it out next to Brittany.

"Whoa, backpack attack!" she joked as papers and notebooks piled up. "Look at all that stuff!"

I snatched up my cell phone. "Nope, nobody's there," I said in disappointment. "And there are zero messages."

"Nothing from Sophie?" Ashley asked. She took off her dress and carefully slipped it on the hanger.

I shook my head. "Or Malcolm. And he promised to call if he talked to her."

"Sophie's not talking, period," Brittany said. She and Lauren knew all about what happened at the mall. "I tried to explain things to her yesterday, but she totally froze me out."

"Check your E-mail," Ashley suggested, pulling on some capris and a tank top.

I crossed my fingers and hurried over to my computer. "Nothing," I reported. "Oh, no—Sophie wiped me off her Buddy List!"

"Ooh, that's harsh!" Brittany declared.

"But it's my fault," I admitted. "I mean, she thinks I stole her boyfriend!"

"So does my mom." Lauren gasped and her face turned pink. "Oh, no! I didn't mean to tell you that, Mary-Kate!"

"But . . . why does your mother even know about this?" I asked.

Lauren's face grew even redder. "My mom saw your mom at the nail salon yesterday. And your mom told mine that you had a great new boyfriend."

Lauren paused and bit her lip.

"I get the feeling there's more," Brittany said.

Lauren nodded. "Your mom said he broke up with a girl so he could date you," she told me.

I closed my eyes. "Is that all?" I asked.

"Yes, except . . ."

I opened my eyes.

"Except a bunch of other kids' mothers were at the salon and they heard everything," Lauren said reluctantly.

"Oh, no, now the whole town knows!" I cried.

"This is definitely getting out of control," Brittany said.

"It's a major nightmare!" I said, taking off my dress. "Sophie won't talk to me or Malcolm and he's *so* upset."

I yanked on a T-shirt and jeans. "The whole

world thinks I broke them up! Nobody'll listen to us. I don't know what to do!"

"There must be some way to straighten this out," Lauren said.

"Right," Brittany agreed. "Let's think—we need a plan."

"I have an idea," Ashley said. "Stop stressing, Mary-Kate. I'll be right back."

Ashley dashed out of the room and was back in five seconds with her cell phone. "*I'm* going to call Sophie," she announced.

"Good idea," Brittany told her. "If she has caller I.D., she won't hang up on *you*."

"I hope not," Ashley said. "If I can keep her on the phone, maybe I can talk her into seeing Malcolm or Mary-Kate."

I watched anxiously as Ashley punched in Sophie's number.

"It's ringing . . . Sophie? It's Ashley—don't hang up!" Ashley rattled out the words. "No, don't! Please! This is important—you have to listen!"

I held my breath.

"Uh-huh," Ashley said into the phone. "Okay."

I let my breath out. Sophie didn't hang up—yet.

"But, Sophie, it's not what you think, it really

isn't," Ashley said. "Don't you want to know the truth?"

I squeezed my eyes shut and crossed my fingers.

"Please, just let Mary-Kate explain!" Ashley begged. "Let me give her the phone right now!"

I took a deep breath and held my hand out for the phone.

Ashley shook her head at me. "Okay," she said to Sophie. "You will? Promise? Maybe? Okay, bye, Sophie."

"I thought she was going to talk to me!" I cried. "What happened?"

"She had to go somewhere. Besides, she wants to think about it," Ashley told me. "She said she might come by the house this afternoon."

"*Might?*" Brittany asked.

"I tried to get her to promise, but she wouldn't," Ashley said.

"At least she's thinking about it. Thanks, Ashley," I said. "Now let's hope she shows up!"

The doorbell rang at three that afternoon. Keeping my fingers crossed that it was Sophie, I rushed downstairs and flung open the door.

Will Foster stood on the porch.

"Hi, um, Will," I said. I tried not to sound disappointed. "What's going on?"

I suddenly noticed the worry in his brown eyes. He was upset.

"I just . . ." Will paused. "The thing is, you said you'd stop by my house. But you never did."

Oh, no! I groaned to myself. The Sophie-Malcolm disaster made me totally forget Will!

"I know, I . . . it's . . ." I stammered. I never really said I'd go to his house. But that didn't matter. He was still hurt. "It's been a really crazy week."

My feeble excuse obviously didn't fool Will. Blushing, he looked me straight in the eye.

"Listen, Mary-Kate, I thought you liked me," he said. "I need to know. Do you?"

"Will . . ." I hesitated. I didn't want to hurt his feelings. What should I say?

chapter fourteen

"**I** *do* like you, Will," I said. I stepped onto the porch and faced him. "But the truth is, I don't like you as a boyfriend."

There, I thought. *Now he knows*. And if he hates me, it's my own fault.

Will didn't look angry. But he did look sad. "I guess my friends were right," he murmured. "They didn't believe it, even after that night at Click."

"I'm sorry, Will," I told him. "I mean that."

"But I don't get it, Mary-Kate. Why did you invite me over and act so nice and all?"

We sat down on the steps and I told him about George. And my lie about having a new boyfriend. Then how I had to find one and how Will just wasn't right after all.

"It wasn't your fault," I told him. "You just

didn't fit the guy I made up. Anyway, I'm really, really sorry. I didn't mean to fool you and hurt your feelings like this."

"It's okay," Will said, standing up. "I mean, I'm not happy about it, but at least I know now. Thanks for being up front with me. Maybe we could be friends? Have lunch some time?"

"You got it!" I said."

I couldn't believe how nice he was being! I knew he was still sad, but he felt better knowing the truth.

And I felt better telling it.

We talked for a few more minutes, then Will left. As I turned toward the door, I spotted a girl with red hair coming down the sidewalk.

Sophie!

I ran out to the sidewalk and practically dragged her into the house.

"You have to listen to me!" I exclaimed, pulling her into the living room. "I know what you think, but you're wrong!"

Sophie crossed her arms. "Okay, I'll listen. For a minute anyway."

I started at the very beginning, with George and the wedding. By the time I got to the part about Malcolm and the mall, Sophie was totally fascinated. And horrified.

"I've been crying myself to sleep, Mary-Kate!" she said. "I thought Malcolm was cheating on me!"

"I know and I feel awful about it!" I cried. I couldn't believe how much I'd hurt her. "I feel awful about everything! I made a huge mistake and everybody got hurt but me. Will and you and Malcolm and Ashley. . . ."

And Mom, too, I realized. *I've got one more thing to do.*

And it's going to be the hardest of all.

"So anyway, I'm sorry, Mom."

Mom came home a few minutes after Sophie left. I took a deep breath, went into the kitchen, poured two glasses of water, and told her everything. She was watching me now across the table, looking sad.

"I never meant for things to get so crazy," I added, wishing she would say something. *Anything!*

Mom took my hand. "I'm sorry, too, Mary-Kate," she said. "You shouldn't have lied to me that way. But you know, it's partly my own fault."

"*Your* fault? How?"

"I put you in a very difficult position," Mom

admitted. "I had no right to meddle in your love life and force George on you that way. It wasn't fair."

Mom squeezed my hand and smiled. I smiled back. I was so lucky to have such a fair-minded mom.

"Anyway, you've done the right thing and cleared the air," Mom finished. "I can see you've learned your lesson the hard way. So I'm proud of you."

"Thanks, Mom."

She lifted her water glass. "And now, on with the wedding!"

"On with the wedding!" I echoed. We clinked glasses.

I felt so much better. It was like all my lies weighed about fifty tons, and I'd finally gotten out from under them!

"Jeanine and James are actually married!" I exclaimed to Ashley that night as we went into the reception hall. "Wasn't the ceremony cool? It was so exciting walking down the aisle!"

"Everything was perfect," Ashley agreed. "And I loved the vows they wrote to each other. They were so sweet."

"I know. Aunt Katherine was crying."

"I saw tears in *your* eyes, too, Mary-Kate," Ashley teased.

"You're right," I admitted. I glanced around the hall. There were baby roses everywhere, in pots, in topiaries, and in the middle of the linen-covered tables.

On a long table at the front was the cake—five tiers covered with butter-cream frosting crowned with a bouquet of spun-sugar roses.

"The Cakery did a great job," Ashley said as we checked out the cake.

"So did you," I told her. "You're the one who told Ava about it."

"And I'm glad she did," Ava said, coming up to us in a shimmering silvery dress. "Thank you again, Ashley. For the place cards, too. I was so relieved to see those *e*'s!"

"You're welcome. So was I." Ashley laughed.

Ava moved away and I nudged my sister in the arm. "I see a summer job in your future!" I said.

The band struck up a tune and everyone clapped as Jeanine and James entered the hall. Jeanine was beautiful in her white silk dress, and James looked handsome in a black tux and crisp white shirt.

A spotlight hit the couple, and they began dancing together.

"By the way," Ashley whispered to me, "did you see Obnoxious George?"

"George Harris? No! Where is he?" I glanced around, but the hall was dim except for the spotlight.

"Relax, I haven't seen him," Ashley told me. "I was just wondering."

How weird, I thought. I'd totally forgotten about George Harris! And he was the reason for all my lies. But it didn't matter anymore. Not even George could spoil this day for me!

The dance ended and the lights came up. Ashley went off to find Aaron, and I checked out the tables until I found my place card.

A tall blond guy was in the chair next to mine. "Hi," I said as I sat down. "I'm Mary-Kate Olsen."

He stared at me, then slowly smiled.

He's really cute, I thought, noticing the dimple in his cheek. Maybe Brittany was right about guys and weddings!

"Is that really you, Mary-Kate?" the guy asked, peering closely at me.

I peered back just as closely. Blue eyes. Thick blond hair. No way! I thought.

"George?" I cried. "George Harris?"

"Mary-Kate?"

"Yes!"

"Yes!" George grinned.

I burst out laughing. "I don't believe this. You're so, um, different-looking!"

"You, too."

I waited for him to joke about my dress or hair—that's what the little George would have done. But the grown-up George just kept smiling at me.

"So how was boarding school?" I asked. "Your mom said you just got back."

"It was good. I made some great friends," he said. "And it was close to Boston—that was fun."

As George started telling me about going into Boston, his little sister, Regina, raced up to the table. "Where's Mommy, George?" she demanded. "I'm hungry!"

"Mommy's over there," George said, pointing. His mother, my mother, and Aunt Katherine were talking together on the other side of the hall. "But she doesn't have the food, Regina. The waiters are going to bring it out in a little while."

"But I'm hungry *now*!" the little girl whined.

"So am I, kiddo," George whispered to her. "Let's go see what we can find in the kitchen. Be right back, Mary-Kate."

I nodded. I still couldn't get over how much he changed!

A few minutes later George came back with a bag of crackers. "Want some?" He held the bag out to me. Munching crackers, we started talking like old friends. George was so different from the way I remembered him! He wasn't obnoxious at all. He was nice and smart and funny. And, oh yeah, cute!

"This is so weird," I told him. "I mean, I was positive you'd be the same George I knew eight years ago!"

"You mean a pain in the neck?" he asked.

"Right." I grinned. "Anyway, I tried everything to get out of being your date tonight. And I mean *everything*!"

"You want to know a secret? *I* did the same thing!" George whispered. "When you were eight, I thought you were a pretty big pain, too!"

We both burst out laughing again.

"Hey, would you like to dance?" George asked as the band started up again.

"Sure!" The music kicked up—loud and fast! "Let's dance!" I cried.

I pulled George onto the dance floor. Ashley and Aaron joined us and we all danced together.

The dance floor filled up with all the bridesmaids and ushers, parents and kids. Soon Ashley and I were jumping and swinging in the middle of a clapping crowd! A photographer wandered around, snapping shots of everyone.

"See that blond guy?" Ashley cried to me over the music. She nodded toward George, who was dancing with his little sister. "Is that who I think it is?"

"Yes, and guess what? He's not obnoxious anymore!" I laughed.

As I spun around, I saw Jeanine and James heading toward us, holding hands. "Hey, can the bride and groom get a picture taken with their favorite cousins?" James asked.

"We want a really good one of just the four of us," Jeanine said. "You guys did so much to make our wedding special."

"You two are the best!" Ashley declared as we put our arms around the couple.

"And that's the truth!" I grinned, and the photographer snapped the shot.

Find out what happens next in

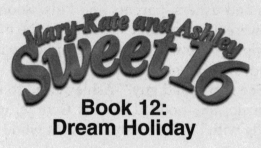

Book 12:
Dream Holiday

"It's true, Ashley," our new friend, Nancy, said. "Prince Stephen of Montavan is spending his Christmas vacation at Snowbeam."

My sister, Mary-Kate, gripped my hand. "Are you kidding me?" she cried. "Prince Stephen is staying here?"

Nancy laughed. "You haven't heard? The whole resort is talking about it."

I grabbed a chair and sank into it. Prince Stephen of Montavan! Here! In this very resort. Skiing on the same snow as me! Riding the same lifts! Snacking at the same snack bars . . .

Everybody knew who Prince Stephen was. His father, Prince Rudolph, ruled the tiny European kingdom of Montavan. His mother, Princess Anne, was American and a former actress. Prince Stephen was a year older than me, seventeen, and went to the Northrup Academy, a prep school in Massachusetts. His whole life was totally glamorous.

"Have you seen him?" I asked Nancy.

"No," she replied. "At least, not that I know of. Nobody knows what he looks like."

"That's right," Mary-Kate said. "His picture has never been published. His parents are totally terrified of kidnappers."

"But we know his name," I protested. "Maybe we could look up his room number or something and call him."

Nancy snorted. "Are you kidding? I'm sure he's got all kinds of security around him. And anyway, he's not using his real name. I heard he uses an assumed name when he goes on vacation to avoid publicity."

"But there must be a way to figure out who he is," I said. "I mean, he's a prince! Doesn't it seem like it should be obvious?"

"I don't know," Mary-Kate said. "His mother's American and he goes to school here, so he doesn't have an accent."

"Believe me, everybody at Snowbeam is trying to pick him out," Nancy said. "But so far, if the prince has left his condo, nobody has noticed."

I still couldn't believe Prince Stephen was so near. I had to meet him. I just had to! How could I spend two weeks so close to a real live prince and not meet him? I'd never forgive myself if I missed this chance.

"If only we could get invited to the Christmas Eve party somehow," Mary-Kate said. "The prince is sure to be there—and then we could meet him!"

"I like the way you think, Mary-Kate," I said. "But Christmas Eve is more than a week away. Our vacation will be half over by then! I don't want to wait that long. If we could make friends with the prince before the party, he could bring us with him as his guests!"

"You're both dreaming," Nancy said. "How are you going to get invited to the party? And how are you going to meet the prince if you can't figure out who he is?"

"I don't know," I said. "But there's got to be a way."

"Look, it's a beautiful afternoon," Mary-Kate said. "Why don't we hit the slopes?"

"Good idea," Nancy said. "I'll bundle up the kids I'm baby-sitting and meet you outside in half an hour."

"Sounds good," I said. "Who knows—while we're out there, maybe we'll run into Prince Stephen!"

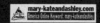